It's Not That Simple, Natty Rose

Dr. Tim Rice

(Timothy S. Rice, D. Min., LPC)

Published by
Rocking R Ventures, Inc.
104 Goss Street
Epworth, GA 30541
www.rockingrventures.com
www.homeschoolpsych.com

Chapter 1

Natalia Rose Sanders had never seen so many people her own age in the same place at the same time. The auditorium buzzed with the sound of 150 college students, each carrying a new book bag and looking for a seat, while trying to appear cool, comfortable, and mature.

Natalia hoped she did not look as scared as she felt. She wanted to shout, "I made it!" one second and, "I want my momma!" the next. Instead, she took a deep breath, said to herself, *I've got this,* and made her way down one of the stairways that divided the auditorium into three sections. She chose the middle seat in the middle row in the middle section of the auditorium. Natalia sat down and, feeling awkward, checked her schedule. It read:

PSYCH 1101
Weber
Mon 8:50am
Boring Auditorium A

The E. G. Boring Auditorium was part of the Psychology and Literature Complex, the newest building at State University. The stadium style seating gave each seat an unobstructed view of the stage and lectern and the jumbo state-of-the-art video monitor. It reminded Natalia of an IMAX theater, but instead of cup holders, each seat had a small folding desktop for writing.

Introductory Psychology was required for Early Childhood Education majors at State University. Natalia had wanted to be a 1st grade teacher for as long as she could remember.

She looked around the auditorium and noticed a few familiar faces from the dorm. She saw her suitemate, Gladys, in the top row, all the way against the auditorium wall – as far from the lectern as possible. Natalia waved, but Gladys didn't seem to notice.

She's different, Natalia thought as she recalled meeting the girl who shared her bathroom.

Natalia's half of the "suite" was about the size of her bedroom back home. It had a bed, desk, and dresser, and was separated from Gladys' half by a door, the bathroom, and another door.

Natalia's dad and little brother had each made four trips carrying boxes and plastic tubs of clothes, books, and other necessities to the second floor of Laurel Dorm. Mrs. Sanders had unpacked her daughter's clothes while Natalia had hung her favorite pictures in just the right places. Mr. Sanders had sat on the edge of the bed, looking uncomfortable, while Natalia's little brother had played a game on their mom's phone.

Natalia knew that most girls requested their suitemates, but Natalia hadn't known anyone to request. She wasn't hoping for a new best friend, just a nice girl to talk to.

Natalia had first seen Gladys through the open doors of the bathroom that connected their rooms. She had tossed a green duffle bag on the bed, and suddenly looked back at Natalia. Her hair was jet black and hung straight over her forehead. She wore heavy black eyeliner, and had five earrings in the ear that Natalia could see. Her torn jeans had ridden low on her hips, held up by a wide black belt barely doing its job.

Natalia had smiled and said, "Hi. My name is Natalia, but my friends call me Natty Rose."

Gladys had taken off her leather jacket and had tossed it, too, onto the bed. "I'm Gladys," she had said.

Her arms were covered with tattoos. Natalia had tried not to stare.

The door near the stage clicked open, interrupting Natalia's thoughts. The auditorium became quiet as four girls and three guys filed in and sat in folding chairs on the right of the stage. They looked older and seemed uncomfortable being the center of attention.

They must be the teaching assistants.

Right away, Natalia noticed a guy at the end of the row with long blond hair and a navy blue blazer.

He's cute.

She watched as he adjusted his blazer and ran his fingers through his hair. When he looked at his phone, Natalia checked hers one more time.

Ringer off. Check.

The last thing she wanted was for her phone to ring during class. The week after Natalia had gotten her first phone, she had forgotten to turn it off during church. After all, who would call at 12:05 on a Sunday afternoon during Pastor Blackmore's invitation for people to be saved? A wrong number. Natalia had thought she would die from embarrassment at age sixteen over a wrong number.

She noticed there was one missed call – from her mom.

Mom! Really?

Natalia's transition to State U. was hardest on her mom. She had wanted Natalia to go to Temple Bible College. Temple Bible College was known as the place to go to find a husband – a future pastor or missionary or music minister.

Temple Bridal *College.*

Her mom thought Natalia would make a good pastor's wife. There was an unstated expectation that Natalia would get married and start having children soon after she started dating.

When Natalia had announced that she was considering State U., her mom had made a list of the pros and cons. There were zero pros and one big con – the whole godless, humanistic, anti-Christian, politically correct, pro-gay and abortion rights culture. It was also 300 miles from home.

You've got this, she told herself again as she opened her notebook and waited.

At 8:50am precisely, the heavy metal door to the right of the stage snapped open with a loud click. Every head turned to look at the shaft of light and the man who stepped onto the stage.

Dr. Ernst Weber was a tall man and he moved with long, confident strides. If Natalia had seen him on the street, she would have guessed he was a professor. From twenty rows up, Natalia could see that his hair was perfect. His khaki pants and oxford shirt were crisply pressed. His herringbone tweed jacket even had elbow patches.

He stood at the lectern, tapped his tablet, adjusted his glasses, and began to speak. He did not smile and he did not look up.

"I am Dr. Ernst Weber. This is Psychology 1101– Introduction to the Brain and Behavior." His accent made it sound like he had said, "I am Dr. Veeber. Introduction to zee brain and behavior."

Dr. Weber continued, "If you are supposed to be in English 1101, you should be in auditorium B, the King English Auditorium, on the other side of the complex."

There were giggles as two students put their pens, notebooks, laptops, and cell phones back into their new backpacks, and made their way to the top of the auditorium, looking as though they wished they were invisible. As if on cue, the metal door at the back of the auditorium opened and three misplaced students arrived from English class. There was more laughter as the new arrivals, looking equally embarrassed, quickly found seats near the top of the auditorium.

Almost as embarrassing as your phone ringing while the choir softly sings Jesus is Calling, thought Natalia.

She turned back to see Dr. Weber looking up and smiling as the late arrivals found seats. His grey beard and broad smile made him look wise and warm, not at all like his reputation.

He doesn't seem so bad.

"As I was saying, this is Psychology 1101, Introduction to the Brain and Behavior. For most of you, this is your first class at State University. On behalf of the University, welcome. Today you begin a journey – a journey through the discoveries and ideas that shaped civilization and guided human history. It is my goal, like every professor here, to tell you the truth and to teach you how to think."

Natalia took notes. *Truth. How to think.*

"You are all smart and promising undergrads. Every one of you graduated in the top 10% of your high school class. About 1/3 of you graduated in the top 2% of your class."

Natalia graduated at the absolute top of her class.

First in a class of one.

"The registrar tells me there are 6 valedictorians, 18 salutatorians, and 2 National Merit Scholars in the room this morning. The registrar also tells me that a few of you, two to be exact, graduated from 'homeschool or other.'"

Natalia thought, *Don't blush! Don't squirm!*

She joined the other students and looked around, as if to get a glimpse of a real live homeschooler.

Denim jumper and long braided hair anyone?

Natalia had mixed feelings about all the times she and her mother had worn matching handmade jumpers and braided their hair and wrapped it tightly in buns. When she was young, she had wanted to dress just like her mom. She did not want that any more.

Dr. Weber continued, "For many of you, the journey can only begin in earnest when you let go of old ideas and old ways of thinking. Some of you may still cling to some type of religious fundamentalism forced on you by your parents. The Quran, the Torah, and the Bible say God did it all – simple. Well, it's just not that simple."

I've heard that before.

Natalia felt uncomfortable but tried not to let it show.

Dr. Weber paused and looked around the auditorium.

"It is my job, as a scientist, to strip away religious superstitions, to expose them, and to make them seem silly – which they are – rather than discussable – which they are not. Psychology class, more than any other you will take at State University, proves that all religions, Christianity in particular, are delusional. They are exploitative, controlling, inhibitive, and oppressive systems of control. It's my hope that very soon you will grow up and grow out of those old ideas."

Oh my goodness.

"In this class, and at this university, we pursue truth without superstitious baggage. Faith is belief despite the lack of evidence. Here, we require evidence."

Natalia knew that it was important to take good notes, but she didn't know what else to write.

"Science has made it unnecessary to believe in a creator. We've been liberated."

Natalia understood that State U. was a secular liberal arts college, but she didn't expect this attack in the first five minutes of her first class.

Maybe Mom was right.

"Mr. Nathan Sutton, my lead teaching assistant, will come and review the syllabus and the course requirements. Next class I will introduce two giant ideas from the history of psychology – two foundational ideas that have been called a *Dangerous Idea* and an *Astonishing Hypothesis*. Until then, Mr. Sutton."

Dr. Weber closed his tablet, nodded toward the blond boy in the blue blazer, and left the auditorium. The metal door snapped shut behind him.

He did not speak long, but Dr. Weber had made quite an impression.

Chapter 2

When the door snapped shut behind Dr. Weber, the buzz started again with renewed vigor. Nathan Sutton had to say "good morning" three times before he could begin.

I've worked hard for this, he thought as he stood at the lectern that the great Dr. Ernst Weber had just vacated. Not only was Nathan lead teaching assistant, he was also Dr. Weber's lead research associate, and was soon to be Dr. Nathan Sutton. He smiled at the thought.

While Dr. Weber had been speaking, Nathan had studied the faces of the students – especially the redhead in the middle seat.

I hope she's in my study group.

Nathan pulled himself back to reality, took a deep breath, and greeted the class. "Good morning. My name is Nathan Sutton and my team of teaching assistants this semester is seated to my left – Amy Martinez, Jill Cook, Doug Morris, Billy Ray Sweatman, and Ande Phinney."

He remembered to button his blazer now that he was standing. His mother had sent extra cash so he could buy it. He preferred jeans and a t-shirt. He thought that the jacket and khaki pants, oxford button down, and loafers made him look like his father.

Maybe I'll grow a beard.

Nathan continued, "Each of you is assigned to a study group. State University calls them labs, but they are really miniature lectures. Dr. Weber hits the high points, and we fill in the gaps in the small groups. If your registration says Psych 1101 Lab, Martinez, you are in Amy's group on Tuesdays at 6:50pm. If it says Sutton, you are in my group on Wednesdays. If your schedule says Cook, Morris, Sweatman, or Phinney, you are in their group. Each group meets in the basement of the Psych Building, James Hall, room 124. James Hall is on the Quad close to the Library. Read the material before group and be ready to discuss the review questions at the end of each chapter."

Nathan looked forward to being a professor. He loved research and he loved to teach. Unfortunately for Nathan, Dr. Weber still taught lower level classes. At most colleges, professors of Dr. Weber's stature refused to teach introductory classes, leaving the job in the hands of eager teaching assistants. Nathan also looked forward to defending his dissertation, getting published, and working toward tenure.

Dr. Nathan Sutton.

"You'll notice on your syllabus that 25% of your course grade comes from research participation. That means that 25% of your grade is an A if you sign up and participate in one of the research studies conducted by the psychology department. If, for some reason, you do not want to be a part of research," he shrugged his shoulders to emphasize how crazy that was, "you can read 5 articles from peer-reviewed psychology journals and write a 500 word APA formatted summary of each."

He paused and wagged his head as he had practiced. "You don't want to do that." The class laughed politely.

Because we really need subjects.

"Participating in research is interesting and important. Writing summaries of journal articles is not. The sign-up sheets will be at your first study group. If any of you are sophomores or above, we also need research assistants – people to take surveys and people who are good with babies to work in what we call the 'Baby Lab'. Research assistants receive a small stipend."

He held his thumb and forefinger close together and said, "And I do mean *small*." He got another polite laugh from the class.

Chapter 3

Natalia took her turn holding open the heavy fire door at the back of the auditorium as her eyes adjusted to the morning sun. Before class, it had been foggy and quiet, and there had not been many people out yet. After class, the dew sparkled in the light, and the sidewalks were packed with college kids texting and talking on their phones.

Natalia felt a sense of relief that she had her first college class behind her, though it was not really her first. In her senior year of high school, she had been dual enrolled in the community college. Officially, Natalia was already a sophomore.

Natalia hoped that she was in Nathan Sutton's study group. She checked her schedule. It read:

PSYCH 1101 LAB
Sutton
Wed 6:50pm
James Hall 124

Natalia smiled.

Research assistant? Why not? I'm good with babies and I need a job.

She felt her phone vibrate and knew, without looking, that it was her mom.

"Hi, Mom," she answered.

"Hi, Natty Rose."

Her mom and her dad and her best friend, Rachel, as well as most of the people at church, called her Natty Rose as if it was a compound first name – like Betty Sue or Mary Beth. Her annoying 8-year-old brother called her Gnat. "With a G," he explained, because it "bugged" her.

Her mom continued, "I couldn't wait to call. What do you think so far? Is college wonderful? How was class? Tell me everything."

Natalia had said that she liked State U. because it had the best teacher education program, but it wasn't that simple. If Temple Bible had had a better teacher education program, she still would not have chosen it. Even though her best friend went to Temple and it was closer to home, she did not want to go there. The main thing she did not like about Temple Bible College was the rules. It had a strict student code of conduct. Women were not allowed to wear pants or earrings or to paint their fingernails. At Temple, not only was jazz, rock, pop, and country music prohibited, so was contemporary Christian music. Movies were taboo, too – even *The Little Mermaid*, Natalia's favorite.

"It's fine, Mom, but I can't talk now. I have to find my next class. Can I call tonight?"

Natalia knew that her next class, American Literature and Writing, was in the older section of campus, known as the Quad. However, she wanted to enjoy the walk without answering a million questions.

"Oh." Her mom sounded disappointed. "Call between six and seven o'clock while your brother is at soccer practice and you can tell me everything. Okay?"

"Okay, Mom. Love you. Bye."

Natalia had been given her first phone when she turned sixteen and started driving. The rule was that she had to call or text her mother when she arrived at each destination. If she went to the bank, post office, and grocery store, she had to let her mother know that she had made it safely to the bank, the post office, and the grocery store.

Does she expect me to text her when I get to class?

Natalia slowed her pace as she approached the Quad.

One of the things that attracted Natalia to State University – besides that it was not Temple Bible College – was the Quad, or the Liberal Arts Quadrangle, as it was officially known. The Quad was a long, rectangular, park-like courtyard lined on three sides by collegiate gothic styled buildings – the oldest buildings on campus. There was a round fountain in the center of the Quad and wide brick walkways that crisscrossed the courtyard from old building to old building. The Philosophy, Literature, and Psychology buildings defined the west side of the Quad. The Biology, Chemistry, and Mathematics departments occupied the buildings on the east side of the Quad. The library defined the Quad's southern end and the Arch separated the Quad from the shops, bars, and cars in town to the north.

Last year, when Natalia had come for an overnight visit as a high school senior, the bubbly student guide had led the group of prospective students on a nighttime tour of campus. It was the first time Natalia had seen the Quad. She had thought it looked magical.

The student guide had explained that the State University Choctaws, as they were first known, had played their home football games on the Quad. Today, large oak trees made football impossible, but the Quad was perfect for playing Frisbee, studying, napping, or catching some rays.

It's beautiful and so peaceful.

For many years, the Quad was all there was to State University, and the Arch was the main entrance. The Arch stood at the top of three wide granite stairs, and consisted of three black metal columns topped by a curved dome with the phrase, *"Viam Sapientiae Monstrabo Tibi"* in black metal letters. Natalia had translated the words as, "I will show you the way of wisdom". The student guide had explained the tradition that freshmen had to walk around, not under, the Arch. There was a legend, she had said, that said if a freshman walked under the Arch, they would become sterile and never have children.

I'll wait until next year, just to be safe.

American Literature and Writing was in Porter Hall, across campus, on the Quad, next to James Hall, home of the psychology department. As she approached, Natalia noticed a man with his back to her. He was on one knee tending flowers around the trunk of a large tree. He had snow-white hair and he wore dark green work pants and a matching shirt. As she got closer, she heard him humming a song. She slowed her pace to listen. The tune sounded familiar – but she could not place it.

I know that song, she thought.

He must have sensed that someone was watching him. He turned around and gave Natalia a broad toothy smile. "Good mornin', ma'am," he greeted as he tipped an imaginary hat. The patch on his shirt said 'Henry'.

Natalia smiled herself at the warmth of his greeting. "Hi," she said back. She had passed by lots of people that morning, but Henry was the only one who had said good morning.

Natalia found a bench in the sun near where Henry was caring for the flowers.

I claim this bench as my own! she decided.

She had time before class, so she checked her Instagram and Facebook, and watched people.

I like college.

She recognized Nathan Sutton and his team of teaching assistants walking toward her. She guessed they had offices in James Hall. Nathan had his blazer thrown over his shoulder and was wearing mirrored sunglasses. He was laughing and talking as he walked, and the other TAs formed a moving semi-circle around him to hear what he said.

He's like a celebrity.

As they neared, Henry stood, wiped his hands, and greeted them all warmly. She could not hear what they said without looking like she was eavesdropping, but she did manage to hear Henry say, "I'm praying for you guys."

Nathan said, "See you later, Box."

Box?

Nathan turned his head slightly in her direction before he led his entourage into the Psychology building.

Did he just look at me?

When class began, she had a hard time focusing. English grammar was her specialty and Natalia was very well read. She could diagram sentences in her sleep, and she had read the assigned books – *The Great Gatsby, The Brothers Karamazov, Crime & Punishment* – while she was still in high school. When Natalia was in 9th grade, her mom had made a list of the 100 novels that every Christian high school student should read. Natalia had read them all – and more.

But that was not why Natalia could not focus. She pretended to pay attention to Dr. Oakes' explanation of the importance of good grammar, but Natalia was thinking about what Dr. Weber had said.

"It's just not that simple."

Those exact words, spoken by her aunt at Natalia's sweet sixteen-birthday party, had caused a big rift in the Sanders family. The party had been a big deal for her mom. She had planned for months, maybe years. She had made the Fellowship Hall in the basement of First Baptist Church look so special with crepe paper and balloons, and matching plates and napkins. The theme had been Victorian debutante, but hadn't ended with Natalia being presented to society in the hopes of finding a husband. Instead, it was a chance to dress up in elegant but uncomfortable dresses, wear hats and gloves indoors, and to sip hot tea with pinkies extended. No boys had been allowed at this debutante party – except for Natalia's dad and annoying little brother. Natalia and her friends had played games and ate finger foods and giggled about boys and getting married someday.

Mrs. Blackmore, the pastor's wife, was the master of ceremonies and had given the first speech. "Family and friends," she had started, "we have gathered here, in God's presence to give thanks for the life of Miss Natalia Rose Sanders, who we all lovingly know as Natty Rose." There had been a few giggles from the younger girls, but Natalia and her more mature friends had known that this was the serious part. "This is a happy day, but it is also a sad day because the little girl we all know and love with the long red hair is all grown up."

Natalia had sighed and thought, *They always mention my hair.*

Natalia's mom had been supposed to give Natalia a red rose and read a Bible verse. But her lip had started to quiver when she gave Natalia the rose, and when she tried to speak, she had burst into tears. Her dad had tissues ready – he had known the tears would flow. Seeing her mom cry had made Natalia cry, and before long, half the room had been wiping away tears.

Besides bringing tissues, it had been her dad's part of the program to give Natalia a ring – a Promise Ring.

He had taken the ring from his jacket, walked to Natalia's table, and placed it on the ring finger of her left hand. He had looked uncomfortable, but he didn't cry. Natalia had felt uncomfortable, but she had not laughed.

She remembered thinking, *You can do this, Dad.*

Her dad was not good at making speeches and he was not comfortable talking about his emotions. He didn't even say, "I love you" very often, but he showed his love by playing with dolls and attending tea parties with Natalia and her friends – both real and imaginary. When Natalia had wanted to learn how to fish, they had went fishing. When she had started playing soccer, he had become a coach.

Her dad had taken a deep breath and said, "This gold ring symbolizes promise. The promise of your mother and me to always be there for you. And it symbolizes your promise to God." Her mom had sobbed louder. "This ring symbolizes purity." Her dad had continued. "Someday you'll replace this ring with another. The engraving says *Pure love waits.*"

That is the closest we've come to talking about sex, Natalia realized as she had listened to her father talk about purity.

Her dad had bent at the waist given Natalia an awkward side hug, said, "I love you, Natty Rose," and quickly returned to his seat, as he wiped something from his eyes. He had looked relieved. Natalia had been relieved, too. Her brother had rolled his eyes and gone back to his electronic game.

The presentation of a new Bible had come last. That was when her aunt had said it. Mrs. Blackmore had explained that the Bible was a light unto Natalia's feet, it was God's Word and God's will for her life, that the Bible was God-breathed and useful for teaching, rebuking, correcting, and training in righteousness, so that she might be equipped for every good work. "The Bible says it and that settles it."

Aunt Marie had leaned close to Natalia and said in a loud whisper, intended to be heard, *"It's not that simple, Natty Rose."*

Natalia had known what she was talking about. Her aunt said she was a Christian, but she believed differently than Natalia's family. Aunt Marie thought it was okay for women to be pastors, for men to marry men, and to drink real wine at The Lord's Supper.

Mrs. Blackmore had continued with the closing prayer as if she hadn't heard it, but everyone had. Mr. Sanders certainly had. Natalia could tell because when she peeked, she had seen her dad, fists clinched, glaring at his sister. Mr. Sanders had suggested that they not invite her to the party. Her parents had argued about it. Mr. Sanders had predicted that his sister would cause trouble, she always did, but Mrs. Sanders had said it would be rude not to invite her.

After the party, there had been another big argument. Natalia had heard it all before. Her dad had said, "How dare you?" and "You're going to respect our beliefs." Aunt Marie had said, "You're filling her head with dogma. Let her do things and ask questions and think for herself."

When Dr. Oakes asked if there were any questions, Natalia realized that she had spent most of class thinking about the party. She did not have any questions.

After class, back in her dorm room, Natalia looked at her promise ring. She loved it. It was beautiful and perfect, but she didn't like the idea of people thinking she was engaged or already married. She did not intend to get married any time soon, but she did not want to look like she was unavailable.

I can stay a virgin without looking like I'm wearing a wedding ring.

She put the ring back in her Little Mermaid jewelry box and made a mental note to wear it when she went home for fall break.

After the hall meeting, the girls from Laurel dorm, still feeling the excitement of the first day of college, had an impromptu dance party that lasted past midnight. Gladys and some other girls sipped schnapps in a room at the end of the hall. A girl with short blonde hair, one of the schnapps sippers, asked Natalia to slow dance. At that point in her life, all of Natalia's slow dancing had been with girls – practice for someday slow dancing with a boy. However, this time, Natalia declined to dance with another girl.

I like boys.

She meant to call her mom, but she forgot.

Chapter 4

The entrance to the first floor of James Hall was up a half flight of wide marble stairs. The basement, where Nathan waited to lead his study group, was not really a basement. It was only halfway below ground and had tall windows that provided him a view of the people as they entered the building. The only reason for someone to come to the psych building on Wednesday evening was for his study group.

Yes! He thought as he watched the red head climb the stairs. *Things are looking up.*

As he did with each of his students, Nathan smiled, offered her a handshake, and said, "Hi, I'm Nathan Sutton."

Great smile. I love green eyes.

She smiled back, offered her hand, and replied, "I'm Natalia Sanders."

"Nice to meet you, Natalia. Take a seat anywhere," he said as he swept his arm toward the many remaining empty chairs. She took a seat in the front row.

Room 125 in James Hall looked old. It still had a chalkboard. The desks had orange plastic seats and chrome legs and faux wood writing surfaces shaped like upside down commas.

The 80s called. They want their desks back.

After he had introduced himself to the last of his students, Nathan told his best joke – the one about the priest, rabbi, and psychology professor. It never failed. He used the clunky grey metal desk like a perch. He leaned back on his arms and stretched out his legs, crossing them at the ankles. He had had to wear slacks and a jacket to Dr. Weber's first lecture, but now he was comfortable in his favorite blue jeans.

Nathan knew that most students in the class were not interested in psychology and they didn't want to be there. They were future doctors and nurses and teachers and were only there because Psychology 1101 was a required class.

He continued, "Since we're going to be spending a lot of time together this semester, let's do an ice breaker exercise and get to know each other. Instead of you introducing yourself to the class, everyone get a partner. Your partner will introduce you. In order for your partner to make that introduction, you will have to tell them things about yourself. We will take ten minutes for you to have a conversation. Take turns asking and telling. Tell things that you wouldn't tell to someone you just met. Not boring stuff."

Nathan had counted and knew that an odd number of students meant he would be someone's partner. So, without seeming eager, he said "Natalia, I can be your partner, since we have an odd number."

Did she see me checking her out on the Quad?

The other students rotated their desks and began their awkward introductions. Nathan hopped down from his perch and sat in a desk next to Natalia. "Ladies first?" he offered as he leaned slightly forward. He had learned to be an active listener in counseling psychology class. He wasn't interested in counseling psychology, but good listening skills were helpful when meeting girls.

"My name is Natalia Sanders," she said, "but I already told you that. My friends call me Natty Rose. I'm left-handed, but you do not have to know me very well to know that. Remember when Dr. Weber said there were two people in class who went were homeschooled?" She leaned in and whispered, "I'm one of them."

Nathan put his hands on his cheeks and opened his mouth and eyes in mock surprise. "No!"

"Yes," she said, "I was homeschooled from kindergarten all the way through high school. I even took college classes at home. I wear jeans and regular clothes when I go out in public, but on Sunday and when I'm alone in my room, I put on homeschooler clothes – long denim jumpers and white tennis shoes. At night I knit scarves and diagram sentences."

"Nice," said Nathan. "Well, I went to a military academy and when I'm alone in my room I put on my uniform and clean guns."

"Are you joking?" she asked as she leaned back and twirled her hair around her finger.

"It's true," he said.

Twirling hair. Good sign.

"The part about wearing my uniform and cleaning guns isn't true, but I did go to military school."

Natalia looked as if she was unsure whether to believe him. "Was your dad in the military?" she asked.

"No." Nathan paused. "I was a trouble maker. My mother and father didn't know what to do with me. I got in trouble in public school and I got in trouble in private school, so my parents sent me to military school."

He did not tell many people about his military school background. When he did, they always looked like Natalia – surprised. From the moment he had graduated high school, he had cultivated the persona of a hip, freethinking, anti-war, anti-establishment, ladies' man kind of guy. He never told anyone the reason he was a troublemaker – that it was the only way he could get his parents' attention. Nathan believed his father cared more about the factory than his own son, and that his mother was too preoccupied with her social calendar and pear martinis to bother about her son.

"Not only was I schooled at home," Natalia continued, "I was born at home – on purpose. I like broccoli and cheese casserole, my favorite color is green, and I love soccer – playing, not watching. And I never got in any trouble."

When she told him that she loved children and wanted to be an elementary school teacher, Nathan thought perhaps he had found his new research assistant.

She has potential.

He asked, "How many credits do you have? Are you still a freshman?"

"No, I got enough to transfer as a sophomore. Your turn. Tell me more about you."

"I was born in Germany. I hate broccoli, my favorite color is blue, and I played midfield at the academy. And I like motorcycles."

"I've never ridden a motorcycle. I want to. I want to go to Germany, too – and France. I haven't been out of state, except to Florida."

When he noticed ten minutes had passed and the other groups were running out of things to say, Nathan returned to his perch on the metal desk and re-convened the class. He pointed in turn to each group for their introductions.

"This is Parker Nelson and he likes to hunt and play lacrosse."

"This is Jeff Price and he used to have a fear of heights but he got over it and has been skydiving six times."

"This is Deb Nichols and she has ADHD and is in pre-med to be a pediatric neurosurgeon."

"This is Kelsey Watkins and she was homecoming queen and class valedictorian.

When it was their turn, Nathan introduced Natalia first. "This is Natalia Sanders. Her friends call her Natty Rose. She's studying to be an elementary school teacher, she plays soccer, and she likes broccoli and cheese casserole. She was homeschooled, so she's really good at knitting scarves and diagramming sentences."

Nathan understood her smile to mean she did not mind a little teasing.

She was still smiling when she said, "This is Nathan Sutton and he will be giving me my grade, so he can make fun of me if he wants." She looked his way and winked. "He plays guitar, he thought about a career in the military, and his eyes are blue. I mean, his favorite color is blue."

She winked at me.

After everyone had been introduced, Nathan skimmed his notes and cleared his throat. "Let's get down to business. What is psychology?" he asked. "It is the study of you and me and us."

Nathan was a good teacher. He was engaging and interesting. He covered each learning objective – psychology's major theories, the uses of psychology, careers in psychology, and psychology as a science – and he made them relevant. He noticed that Natalia took lots of notes. Other students jotted a word or name occasionally, but she seemed to be transcribing his every word. Her attention energized him.

After he had covered everything on the outline, he said, "The last thing we need to do today is talk about signing up for research studies. I'm sure all of you are going to be a subject and participate in the advancement of science instead of reading journal articles and writing boring papers."

He made it seem like a joke, but finding enough volunteers was no laughing matter. They needed subjects. He wished it was mandatory for every student at State U. Instead, he had to put up flyers on bulletin boards and light poles and coerce Psych 1101 students.

Volunteer or get a bad grade. You decide.

"We need subjects for a study of visual discrimination. It takes about 1 hour and there are no known negative side-effects associated with participation."

So many disclaimers.

"Second, we need people to look at images on the computer and rate them. It also takes about 1 hour. The study is about disgust, so you may get disgusted. Third, we need subjects to complete an opinion survey after listening to speakers on campus. There are no known side-effects, but you may hear speech that is offensive, bigoted, and intolerant."

He pointed to a long folding table by the door. "There are sign-up sheets on the table. Come on up. Remember if you are a sophomore or above we have a few paid research assistant positions."

He looked at Natalia and said, "We really need someone who is good with children. Experience with puppets is helpful, but not necessary. Class dismissed."

Nathan kept an eye on the table with the sign-up sheet as he answered questions about the syllabus. It looked like no one slipped out without signing up to be a research subject.

100% participation.

He called to Natalia as she finished writing her name on one of the sheets. "Natalia, if are you looking for a part-time job, think about applying to be a research assistant in the Baby Lab. You could help make important scientific discoveries."

She said, "I was thinking about it. I didn't mention it, but I do have experience with puppet shows, too."

"You may be over-qualified, then," he said. "Do babies like you? If you make the babies cry, that's bad."

"No. Babies like me. They usually get quiet and stare at my hair. What does the job pay?" she asked.

"A pittance," he answered and held his thumb and forefinger close.

"Hmmm. A pittance is not very much." She put her finger to her cheek and looked at the ceiling. "I have to think about that. I will be here on Friday to be in the visual discrimination study. Can I let you know then?"

"Friday is good."

I think she likes me.

Chapter 5

Natalia's phone vibrated at 7:00am. It was her mom.

"Good morning, Natty Rose! How are you? Did you get a wink of sleep last night?

Wink?

The memory of winking at Nathan popped into her mind.

What was I thinking?

Natalia felt embarrassed.

"Good morning, Mom." Natalia said as she stretched and yawned. "I'm fine."

"Are you excited about visiting your new church home away from home?"

Natalia only half-listened as she replayed the conversation with Nathan in her mind.

"You will be the new girl for a change," her mom continued. "Are you nervous?"

Natalia pushed thoughts of Nathan aside. She was feeling anxious, but not because she was the new girl. She was anxious because she had flirted and she was afraid that she would hate Calvary way. And that would upset her mom.

"I'm a little nervous," Natalia answered, "but I'll be fine."

When Natalia had announced that her mind was made up to attend State University, her mom did not mention Temple Bible College again. She had said, "It is your life and your decision, and I support you even if I don't agree." Instead, Mrs. Sanders had set about finding Natalia a good church. She had put it on the prayer chain. She had asked everybody if they knew anyone who knew anything about churches near State University. After much prayerful consideration, she had selected Calvary Way.

"You're going to love it. We're praying for you, dear."

Mrs. Sanders had been very excited about Calvary Way. "It is a short walk from your dorm, so lots of people from school go there. And Brother Haywood – you remember him? He was our minister of music when you were little. Anyway, he was really good, a little too contemporary for my taste, but good. He is the music minister at Calvary Way. And Mrs. Wells, you know, from the benevolence meal ministry? Her granddaughter went to Calvary Way and she said the teacher for the College and Career Sunday school class was good. They even have an AWANA club in case you want to volunteer."

"I probably will like it," Natalia told her mom as she opened her closet and took out a pair of jeans.

Natalia had decided to try Calvary Way – not because it had an AWANA club, not for the Sunday school teacher, and not for the short walk to campus. It was because they dressed casually and had contemporary music. Calvary Way had two worship services. The late service, at 11:00am, was "traditional," which meant traditional music – hymns – and traditional clothes – dresses. The early service, at 8:30am, was "contemporary." It meant getting up early, but it was worth it for some modern music and not wearing a dress.

Priorities.

"I've got to get dressed now, Mom. I'm going to the early service and then I'll check out the Sunday school class. I'll call and tell you all about it later."

"Okay, dear. I love you. Bye."

"Goodbye, Mom. I love you, too." She tossed her phone on the bed and for the first time in her life, Natalia picked out pants to wear to Sunday morning worship. She thought about Nathan. She winked at her reflection in the mirror – to see how it had looked from his eyes. She felt nervous and excited and a little bit silly.

The walk across campus to Calvary Way calmed Natalia. It was easy to find by its tall steeple. It was larger than her church, but it looked familiar. She recognized the scenes from Jesus' life depicted in the stained glass windows, and she recognized the River Jordan painted behind the baptistery. The pews were familiar, too.

Hard.

At home, Natalia would have been the only girl wearing pants and it would have been scandalous. She was relieved to see that at Calvary Way, lots of girls wore pants – some even wore shorts. Natalia saw women wearing leggings and some wore skirts that did not cover their knees.

The congregation at First Baptist was mostly old people. At Calvary Way, there were couples with young children, and teenagers and people Natalia's age. First Baptist Church was a small church in a small town and she knew everyone and everyone knew her. Calvary Way was a big church in a big town – she did not know anyone, and no one knew her.

When she was young, Natalia had thought living in a small town and going to a small church was cool. She had believed that everything revolved around her and everyone really cared when she lost her first tooth. By the time she was 14, it was not cool anymore.

Everyone knows your business.

At First Baptist, the choir was small and the members wore their regular church clothes. They sang hymns accompanied by an organ and piano. At Calvary Way, the choir was large. Its members wore royal purple robes with golden V-neck stoles., and were accompanied by drums and two keyboards and electric guitars. Since everyone was dressed the same, Natalia noticed faces and hair.

That guy in the back looks familiar.

She noticed the sole redhead in the choir – a tall woman in the second row. It reminded Natalia how much she herself stood out because of her own hair.

Carrot top.

When the choir sang *A Mighty Fortress Is Our God,* they gave it a contemporary twist – complete with swaying and clapping and a heavy backbeat and guitar solo.

Why does the devil get all the good music?

Because it was a college town, the sermon on the first Sunday of Fall semester was always about welcoming strangers. All the new students, faculty, and staff from State University had to stand and blush while everyone looked and welcomed them with a round of applause.

Natalia stood halfway up and quickly sat back down.

Awkward.

She had learned at an early age how to behave in church. Sit still. Do not fidget. No smacking your chewing gum. Sit up straight. She knew how to look like she was paying attention while she thought about everything from soccer to makeup to boys. She was an expert at recognizing when the preacher began to wrap up the sermon – that transition from sermon for the saved to altar call for the lost.

"…And what about you, my friend?"

"But unless you know Jesus…"

Sometimes, when the altar call dragged on, Natalia wondered if the pastor had gotten special word from God that she had said or done or thought something bad and that she really needed to kneel at the altar and confess and repent and rededicate.

"This altar is open."

But she was good at resisting the tug.

Hurry so we can get to the restaurant before the Methodists.

It felt odd. Instead of rushing from the worship service to dinner, Natalia went to find her new

Sunday school class, the one her mom had heard so much about.

I hope they have food.

The College and Career Sunday school class met in a large room in the basement.

I'll be the new kid in Sunday school for a change.

The room was warm and inviting. There were couches and soft chairs and a table with coffee and tea and donuts. Two girls, who looked to be Natalia's age, greeted her as she walked in.

"Hi, I'm Phyllis."

"Hi, my name is Debbie."

There was one person in the room otherwise full of college students, who was obviously the teacher. He was wearing a tie and was big and tall and had white hair. Natalia guessed he was at least 60 years old.

That's the man from the choir. I've seen him before.

The man smiled and stuck out his huge, rough hand.

"Hi. I'm Henry Brown."

The size of his hand, plus the effort of trying to remember where she had seen him before, caused Natalia to forget for a moment to introduce herself.

"Oh. I'm sorry. It's just that you look so familiar. I'm Natalia. Natalia Sanders. My friends call me Natty Rose."

"Welcome, Natty Rose. My friends call me Box. I work at State U. Are you a student there? You might have seen me there working around the Quad."

"That's it!" Natalie smiled. "You were taking care of the flowers and humming a song. I heard some students call you Box."

That was the song!

"When I saw you, you were humming that song from church this morning – *A Mighty Fortress*."

"It's my favorite." He had a deep, rich voice. "You heard me practicing; I need a lot of practice. We sing the same songs in both services – contemporary style in the early and traditional at eleven – but personally, I like the contemporary better. I'm more used to the traditional arrangements, but learning a new way helps keep old people like me connected to young people like you." He laughed heartily and motioned to the refreshments.

I like him.

Natalia got a doughnut and found an empty spot on a big couch. Box announced, "Let's get started. Welcome everybody. Welcome back old timers and welcome to all the new members." Natalia was relieved to learn that she was not the only new student.

Box said, "It has been the custom of this class, since I started teaching it 26 years ago, to do two things every single week. First, we pray. We pray because God commands us to pray. Prayer is how we communicate with God. We share our burdens with God through prayer and participate in his works."

He paused and took a sip from his paper cup. His hands were huge and Natalia thought that he must have been a football player or something.

They call him Box, but he is as big as a house.

"Praying is one thing," he continued. "It's the most important thing, but you guys live in a world where the Gospel is under attack, where Christianity is seen as silly. So, the second thing we do in this class is understand why we believe, and why the Christian worldview is not silly but is the most rational and logical explanation for what we see in the world. I understand that it is tough to be a Christian at State U. It is not a friendly place for Christians. No matter how long you've been a Christian or how well your parents and youth pastors prepared you, or how close you walked with the Lord in high school, it is hard defending and living your faith in college."

I've got this, she reassured herself.

Box walked around the room as he continued. "But, you can be confident of this, despite how hard it is out there, Philippians 1:6 says, 'Being confident of this very thing, that he which hath begun a good work in you will perform it until the day of Jesus Christ.' Nevertheless, you must be ready at all times to give a defense for what you believe. You can't hide, but you don't have to go it alone."

Chapter 6

Dr. Weber hurried to the door of the E.G. Boring auditorium. He could still recall details of the fight to name the new auditorium for the great historian of psychology, Dr. E. G. Boring, instead of a corporate donor.

The Home Depot Auditorium, he thought. *Never.*

He pushed hard on the door at 8:50am precisely. It sounded like a gunshot; he liked seeing the students jump. He walked to the lectern and tapped his tablet to open his notes – but he did not need notes. He knew what he was going to say. He had said it all before.

Maybe I should stop teaching.

As the distinguished Wilhelm Wundt, professor of psychology, Dr. Weber did not have to teach anything, and he certainly did not have to teach Psych 1101.

I have tenure.

Teaching had been his first love, but for the past few years, it had not been as much fun and he often thought about giving it up. He could give it all to the teaching assistants. Most professors of his stature did. He kept teaching because he still felt a sense of duty to teach this class, introductory psychology –

the one almost everyone at State University had to take. Students came to college as bigoted, homophobic fundamentalists, and it was his duty to use psychology to open their minds to new ideas and new ways of thinking.

I'm making a difference.

"The history of psychology," he began, "like every science, is punctuated by new theories that revolutionize the way we think about and explain ourselves. These new theories are revolutionary because they challenge the status quo. Copernicus' heliocentric theory was revolutionary because it challenged the idea that Earth was the center of the universe. Two such revolutionary theories from psychology are known as Darwin's *Dangerous Idea* and Francis Crick's *Astonishing Hypothesis.*

"When Darwin wrote *The Origin Of Species*, or more accurately *On The Origin Of Species By Natural Selection, or The Preservation Of Favoured Races In The Struggle For Life*, psychology was in its infancy. Modern scientific psychology started in 1879, at the University of Leipzig."

My alma mater.

"The Wilhelm Wundt chair of psychology at State U. is named in honor of Wundt's role in the founding of modern psychology."

Dr. Weber was proud to follow in Dr. Wundt's footsteps and to hold the chair named in his honor.

"Modern psychology was founded twenty years *after* Darwin published these words in the closing chapter of *The Origin of Species.*"

Dr. Weber tapped his tablet and a quote flashed big on the screen behind him.

In the distant future I see open fields for far more important research. Psychology will be based on a new foundation, that of the necessary acquirement of each mental power and capacity by gradation. Light will be thrown on the origin of man and his history (Darwin, 1859).

Dr. Weber continued, "You have the good fortune to study psychology at a time when Darwin's prediction has come true. Today, psychology – like every other life science – is based on an evolutionary foundation. His idea was called 'dangerous', quote unquote, because it was revolutionary – it explained the human mind not as the crowning achievement of some intelligent designer, but as a product of natural selection."

Dr. Weber knew that if he asked for a show of hands of those who believed in evolution, almost every hand would go up. But if he asked for a show of hands of those who believed that evolution applied to them, that it was sufficient to explain their subjective experience of life, there would be fewer hands raised.

They do not really believe.

"Just a few decades ago, I was an undergraduate at the University of Leipzig. That was long after Darwin published his theory, yet evolution was virtually absent in all of psychology's theories."

People cling to their simple explanations.

"When I came to State U. 26 years ago, evolution wasn't taught at all in lower level psychology courses."

But I changed that.

"Today, however, evolution shines a light on our origin and history, providing a framework for understanding human psychology."

He tapped his tablet and a new quote flashed on the screen.

You, your joys and your sorrows, your memories and your ambitions, your sense of personal identity and free will in fact no more than the behavior of a vast assembly of nerve cells and their associated molecules.

Weber thought, *Pause for effect…*

"This revolutionary idea, from Nobel prize winning biologist Francis Crick, is known as the Astonishing Hypothesis. You are your brain. All mental powers and capacities are the product of the physical brain. You are nothing but a pack of neurons."

Dr. Weber enjoyed seeing students squirm – mouths and eyes wide open in shock and disbelief when he told them they were nothing but packs of neurons.

"Dr. Crick's hypothesis is astonishing not only because it is revolutionary, but because it also contradicts dualism. Renee Descartes, your parents, the Pope, Muslims, Christians, Jews, and spiritualists of all flavors are dualists. They believe humans have two natures. One is physical – the brain and body and neurons. And they believe there is something else, a non-physical nature – a soul, a life force, a ghost in the machine that is *spiritual*, not physical. Descartes believed the soul and the body, the physical and the spiritual, connected at the pineal gland, deep in the brain. Christians believe the soul and body connect in the heart; the ancient Egyptians believed it was in the liver. But we learn from Darwin's idea and Crick's hypothesis that there is no soul, and our brain –like the rest of the body – was designed by evolution."

He paused. *Will there be one this semester?*

Sometimes that was more than students could take. Sometimes, they would raise their hands, and

51

sometimes they would shout out, "That's not true!" He loved when that happened. He loved it because he liked to ridicule and humiliate believers – "faith heads," as he liked to call them. Today he wanted someone to object. He wanted to use his position and authority to crush some stupid little faith head's narrow-minded foolishness. He enjoyed it best when he made them cry.

Anyone?

Sometimes they walked out. It was never quiet when that happened. They slammed closed their books and made their way up the aisle, holding back the tears, and through the heavy metal door.

Grow up.

However, because most students needed to take psychology to graduate, they usually came back.

Last chance.

Dr. Weber was disappointed when no one challenged him. He continued, "The human brain, like the body, is an assemblage of neurological adaptations, designed by evolution to solve the problems of living that our ancestors faced. The human brain evolved to find food and shelter; to identify, attract, and retain mates; to recognize friends and enemies; to avoid predators; to raise offspring; and to survive in a hostile environment. That is why we are said to have Stone Age minds in the modern world."

Dr. Weber knew it was not that simple, but he did not doubt it was true. He understood that modern neuroscience, with all its advances in technology, could not explain how the brain worked. Scientists could not explain how neurons and chemicals and electrical impulses produce the subjective human experience of consciousness, much less the mechanisms by which consciousness evolved.

It takes a great mind to fully understand.

Dr. Weber believed he had a great mind. He could not have earned his reputation as a leader in evolutionary psychology without one.

When they were younger, his wife had told him that he had a great mind. She had said she believed in him – and he had believed her. She also had said she loved him for his mind, and that his good looks were a bonus. He had believed that, too.

"Humans are a young species. The brain evolved into its present form about 200,000 years ago and has changed little since. To understand human psychology, one must ask what life was like for our ancestors. What things were dangerous? What characteristics did our ancestors need to survive and reproduce?"

Is this all there is?

Dr. Weber called himself a satisfied atheist. He was familiar with the arguments that said atheism was empty and that for the atheist, morality and love and beauty were meaningless illusions. Science and reason gave his life meaning, and he was happy – at least, until recently.

"An astonishing hypothesis and a dangerous idea. When these ideas no longer seem astonishing or dangerous, then you can really begin to grasp what it means to study psychology." He tapped his tablet again and the screen went blank.

"Next week we'll look at two more giants from the history of psychology, Sigmund Freud and B. F. Skinner."

He walked across the stage and swung wide the metal door through which he had entered. He paused as the door slammed closed behind him. He enjoyed pausing to hear the buzz erupt after his dramatic exits.

Dr. Weber used to stop on his way back from the auditorium to sit on the bench near the psychology department and appreciate the beauty of the Quad. Sometimes he would think about his wedding near the fountain. He used to enjoy the cool air and the color of the leaves, but now he hardly noticed either – and he certainly did not write love poems anymore.

He did not appreciate much these days. He was just angry. These days, on his way back to his corner office overlooking the Quad, Dr. Weber would think about quitting teaching, he would think about his wife, and he would think about how much he hated Henry Brown.

Distinguished professor Ernst Weber had never liked Henry Brown. He was just another faith head – nice enough, but simple and confused. Over the past two years, his dislike had festered like an untreated, disgusting infection.

I really hate that man.

They had both started at State University 26 years ago. They each held their beliefs dear, Box his Christianity and Dr. Weber his atheism. Once, when Henry Brown asked, "Dr. Weber, do you know Jesus?" Weber had laughed and launched into a tirade about how science had made belief in gods unnecessary and how religious beliefs were byproducts of a hyperactive agency detection device – an evolved drive to find a cause for everything. Since then, they did not speak much. It used to irritate Dr. Weber when Henry would say, "I'm praying for you, Ernst." Now it infuriated him.

He looks safe and friendly, but he is dangerous.

Box was tending flowers and humming. Dr. Weber walked near the edge of the sidewalk hoping that Box would not see him, but it didn't work.

"Hi, Ernst," Box said as he wiped his brow.

"Hello."

"Beautiful day."

"Harrumph! No time. Got to go."

"I'm praying for you, Ernst."

I do not want your prayers.

Chapter 7

"I like college, Mom. I like the girls on my hall and the food is good. When you visit, I can take you downtown. You'll like it."

Natalia talked as she walked back toward campus. She had spent the afternoon downtown, checking out the shops and galleries that lined the streets. She had felt sophisticated drinking her decaf latte at a sidewalk café. Afterwards, in a dress shop where everything was out of her price range, Natalia had tried on a short white dress with a deep V-neck and skinny straps.

Pretty.

Mrs. Sanders said, "I'm looking forward to visiting, dear."

"I got an A on my English lit paper."

"Congratulations, Natty Rose! You were always a good writer."

"It's because you were such a good teacher."

"No, you were such a good student," her mom said.

With the exception of two weeks in Christian school, Natalia had always been homeschooled. Her mom had heard about homeschooling from some families at church and on Christian radio, and she had read some books about it. She had said, "I feel convicted – called by God to homeschool." Natalia's dad said that Natalia was homeschooled even before she was born. Her mom had made him read books to their unborn child. It had made him uncomfortable, but he did it anyway.

Homeschooling was all Natalia knew. Until she was six, she had not thought of it as school. Natalia had played and her mom had read books to her. When Natalia was six years old, her mom had begun to teach math and science, history and Latin, as well as how to diagram sentences. Natalia had studied the Bible and memorized verses for AWANA. Through it all, Natalia had read – either by herself or with one of her parents. Even during summer break and her free time, she had read good books.

Homeschooling, for Natalia, had meant lots of field trips and no TV, and regular errands like trips to Walmart, had been educational opportunities. Homeschooling had meant going to conferences and seminars, joining a co-op and support group, and it meant lots of socialization and play dates with other like-minded homeschool families – mostly Rachel's family.

Her mom had done everything right. She had poured herself into homeschooling, but sometimes she still worried that Natalia and her little brother would turn out to be failures or mass murderers with low SAT scores and no social skills. When they were in middle school, Natalia and Rachel had decided they wanted to go to public school like their friends. Despite her self-doubt, Mrs. Sanders had laughed and said there was "no chance, no way" she would ever put one of her children in the public school. "Just get that idea out of your head, young lady." It was that simple.

"Well," Natalia said, "I think you were a great teacher," and she changed the subject by asking, "What are you making for dinner, Mom?"

"Thank you, dear. To God be the glory. I'm making your favorite – broccoli and cheese casserole." Mrs. Sanders sang the words broccoli and cheese.

"Mmm mmm. I miss your casseroles."

Natalia had not been away from home long enough to really miss her mom's cooking. Her mom was famous back home for her casseroles. Mrs. Sanders made chicken casseroles and tuna casseroles and beef, turkey, and vegetarian casseroles. She made a gluten-free casserole when necessary, and a taco casserole, and one with sweet & sour chicken when she felt adventurous. If company was coming, she made two casseroles, one with meat and one without. If there was a birth, death, adoption, tragedy, or a new church family, the women of First Baptist's benevolence meal ministry delivered casseroles. As the meal ministry's longest serving chairwoman, Natalia's mom had probably made a thousand casseroles. She would say, "Jesus fed the multitudes and I do what I can."

Her had dad joked, "If someone died and your mother didn't make a casserole, are they really dead?"

Natalia's mother asked, "What are your plans for this evening?"

"I'm on my way to the psychology department to be a research subject," Natalia said. "*Very important* research on vision."

Natalia laughed, but her mom did not laugh back.

"Be careful," she warned. "Don't let them brainwash you or anything."

I shouldn't have mentioned it.

Natalia knew how her mom felt about psychology. She did not trust it. Her mom had attended a lecture at a homeschool conference where she had heard that psychology was part of the great seduction of the anti-Christ – that it was a crutch for people hiding from God. She called it psycho-babble. Natalia had thought her mom was overreacting, until she heard Dr. Weber. To date, her explanations of evolution had come from people who did not believe it. But Dr. Weber was so sure.

"I won't let them brainwash me, Mom."

As Natalia approached campus, she saw a crowd of people, mostly guys, drinking beer outside of a pub. The neon sign said *Papa Joe's*. Across the street, at the Arch, there was a commotion.

"I will call you tonight and let you know how it went. There's something going on now and I want to check it out," she said as tapped the end call button.

The commotion was the Cowboy, as everyone at State University knew him. The Cowboy was a street preacher. For the past 26 years, five days a week, two hours a day, rain or shine, the Cowboy preached. Sometimes he preached about Jesus and love and Heaven, but mostly he shouted warnings about sin and death and Hell.

"You need to get saved!" His voice boomed over the bustle of the campus.

He waved the Bible over his head like a lariat. In his other hand, he held a sign. One side read:

HE THAT HATH THE SON HATH LIFE...

The other side finished the verse:

...AND HE THAT HATH NOT THE SON OF GOD HATH NOT LIFE.

Natalia could hear him clearly from across the street.

"You need to get right with Jesus! You sinners! Fornicators! Drunkards! Pornographers! Repent or burn in Hell!"

Most students ignored him.

"TURN OR BURN!"

Sometimes they stopped to listen.

"DO YOU KNOW WHERE YOU WILL SPEND ETERNITY?"

Sometimes they mocked him. Each year for Halloween students scoured local thrift stores for long sleeved white shirts with mother of pearl buttons, bolo ties, pointed toe boots, and white ten-gallon hats to dress like the Cowboy. When he preached at the Arch, *Papa Joe's* offered 2-for-1 drinks. When the news spread on social media that the he was preaching at the Arch, it was called 'a Cowboy sighting,' and a crowd gathered to drink and laugh and hurl insults.

"REPENT!"

The crowd outside *Papa Joe's* looked to be mostly University students. It was the middle of the afternoon, but the Cowboy had been preaching for a while, judging by the way the college boys slurred their insults.

"Hey, Cowboy, why are you so intolerant?"

"Don't be a hater, Mr. Cowboy!"

"Shut your mouth. Nobody cares about your god!"

"Hater! Fool! Where can I get a funny hat like that?"

Natalia felt sad and angry. The Cowboy was not hurting anybody.

Why do they have to be so mean? she wondered.

A few years ago, State University had tried to prohibit the Cowboy from preaching on campus. They could not prohibit his speech, but they did try to restrict it. The university had designated a single free speech zone near the back of the student center. With help from the Association of Christian Attorneys, Cowboy had sued. Elizabeth Weber – lead counsel and wife of distinguished psychology professor, Ernest Weber – had defended the University. She had tried her best, arguing that Cowboy's message was hate speech and that the First Amendment did not protect it, but she lost, and Cowboy was free to preach in any public part of campus. Since then, he moved around. On some days, he preached near the dormitories, some days at the cafeteria, and some days on the Quad under The Arch.

Natalia crossed the street, climbed the marble stairs, and walked wide around the Arch, hoping the Cowboy would not notice.

I wonder if he has a wife and children, she thought as she avoided making eye contact. "You!" he shouted. She knew, without looking, that he meant her. "Do you know JESUS?!"

"Yes, thank you," she said quietly as she hurried past.

Street preachers made Natalia feel uncomfortable – uncomfortable because she did not talk about Jesus very often. The boldest evangelism she had done was when she had handed out Bible tracts on the public beach near summer camp. She believed that what the Cowboy was saying was true, people needed Jesus, but she was uncomfortable with his name-calling, finger-pointing, hell-fire and damnation style.

Not feeling the love, Mr. Cowboy.

The shouts faded as Natalia walked along the Quad. She had a few minutes left before the study. She hoped that Box was there. She wanted to get to know him. Natalia saw him installing short wire fences around the flowerbed at the trunk of a young tree. She noticed that several trees on the Quad had little fences around them.

She waited to call out so she could listen for humming.

"Hi, Box! What song are you humming this week?"

"Oh, hi, Natty Rose," he said as he pushed the fence into the ground with his foot. "It's called, *Oh Happy Day.*"

"I don't know that one."

"I'm not surprised," he laughed. "It's an old negro spiritual – I'm not sure if it's politically correct to say that, though. I call it swaying music. Calvary Way is getting its cultural diversity on."

She smiled.

I could use a little cultural diversity.

"I can't wait to hear it," she said. "Why are you putting fences around the trees?"

"There's a home football game this weekend. We install these fences because sometimes, when we win, things get out of hand. Sometimes, when we lose, too." He laughed and shrugged. "Alcohol. It makes people crazy. Why are you on old campus in the middle of the afternoon? To ask me about fences?"

"No, I'm here to be part of an 'important' scientific psychology study," she said, as she made quotation marks in the air. "But I do have a question. Why do they call you Box?"

He laughed. It was warm and made Natalia smile.

"Now that's a story, young lady. Two stories, to tell the truth. Let's sit down," he said, pointing to Natalia's favorite bench.

"Now this may sound unbelievable, but I was named after my great-grandfather, Henry Moses Brown. He was a plantation slave in South Carolina. When his wife and children were sold to another plantation, he was heartbroken – he couldn't live without them. So he made a plan to run away. He packed himself in a wooden crate and shipped himself to Pennsylvania." Box laughed again. "He almost died, but he made it. People started calling him Box."

"Really?" asked Natalia.

"It's true," said Box. "He worked hard and saved money and was able to buy freedom for his wife, my great-grandmother, and one of his sons, who turned out to be my grandpa."

"Wow! What a story," said Natalia.

"I'm happy that they didn't call him Crate." Box laughed and slapped his knee. "But there's another reason they call me Box. When I was young, I was angry and liked to fight. My mom took me to a gym where I learned to box. She wanted to channel my anger into something productive, but I just liked fighting. You probably don't know that State U. had a boxing team a long time ago. I was on it."

Natalia was surprised. "You don't seem like a fighter."

"I fought all the time. But since I found Jesus," he said, "I don't fight with my fists anymore. I fight against the powers of this dark world and against the spiritual forces of evil in the heavenly realms."

"Ephesians 6:12," said Natalia.

"That's right," he said. "For our struggle is not against flesh and blood. I fight on my knees these days."

"That's a great story. Thank you for telling it," said Natalia.

Box laughed again. "You're welcome. What time are you supposed to be a human guinea pig – I mean, what time are making your *important* contribution to science?"

"A human guinea pig. That's funny," she said as she checked the time on her phone. "When I was three years old, I begged my dad to let me have a pet guinea pig. He said no, but he talked my mom into letting me have a puppy. I named him Patches. I had Patches for two days when I guess I decided to join Patches for supper. I put my face in his bowl while he was eating and he bit me on the lip. See, I've got a little scar on my lip as a reminder of Patches and to never eat out of a dogs' bowl."

They both laughed.

Natalia said, "I'd better go now. Human guinea pigs must not be late. See you Sunday." She turned and waved as she jogged up the stairs to the William James Psychology building.

The handwritten sign on the door of room 121 read:

VISUAL DISCRIMINATION STUDY

Do I knock?

There were two guys and two girls sitting at a table. Natalia guessed they were also volunteers. They were not talking and did not turn around when she entered. They seemed focused on the far side of the room, where a computer monitor sat on a large metal desk. Natalia took a seat near the door. Two more guys and another girl that she did not recognize entered and sat in the remaining chairs, and joined the others staring at the blank screen.

To break the ice, Natalia said, "So, it looks like we're human guinea pigs." No one laughed - not even to be polite.

Awkward.

After a few minutes, a young woman came in through a different door from an adjoining room. She wore a white lab coat and black glasses and her hair was in a bun.

I would look cute in a white lab coat.

"Hi," she said, adjusting her glasses, "My name is Jill Cook, and I'll be conducting today's study."

Jill explained that they were assembled for a psychological experiment on visual discrimination, that there were no known side-effects from participation, and that they could withdraw at any time.

"At the end of your participation in today's study, you will meet with the senior research assistant who will debrief you and answer your questions about today's study."

I hope it's Nathan. I'd like to see him again.

Jill adjusted her glasses and then pushed a button on the monitor. It flickered to life, showing a white background and four black vertical lines. On the left of the screen, one of the lines was apart, separated from the others, and had the word 'control' printed below it. On the right, close together, were three lines of varying lengths with the letters A, B, and C printed below them.

Papa Bear, Momma bear, and Baby Bear. Natalia thought.

Jill explained, "Your task is simply to judge the length of the lines that I will show you. We will go around the room and, one at a time, you will indicate which of the lines on the right – A, B, or C – is the same length as the control line on the left."

Baby Bear line is just right.

"Are there any questions?"

Is that it?

There were no questions. The other guinea pigs looked bored.

"Very well. Here is trial #1." Jill tapped the keyboard and a new set of lines appeared. She pointed at the screen and asked, "Which of lines marked A, B, or C is the same length as this line? We'll start with you."

Jill motioned toward Natalia, who looked at the other guinea pigs to see if they thought this was as weird as she did.

It's obviously B.

"Momma Bear, I mean B. Line B."

Then the guy to her left went next. "It's B."

Then the girl to his left said, "It's B."

And around the table it went until each subject had correctly answered, "B."

Jill tapped the keyboard and displayed a new set of lines. She pointed to the girl on Natalia's right and repeated the instructions from her script. "Which of lines marked A, B, and C is the same length as this line? We'll start with you this time."

"It's C," she said.

Natalia said, "It's C."

"C."
"C."
"C."

Natalia thought that as a study on visual discrimination, the lines would eventually get more difficult to judge – like an eye chart where the letters got smaller and smaller at the bottom. But trial after trial after trial, it was perfectly clear which line was the correct choice. The only thing that changed was which subject went first – and consequently, which went last.

Important research?

"It's A."

"A."
"A."
"A."
"A."

Then something strange happened. The guinea pig on Natalia's left went first and got it wrong. He said "C," when the right answer clearly was B.

What? Did he just say C?

Natalia almost laughed out loud.

Is he playing a joke on poor Jill?

Natalia smiled and looked to see Jill's reaction, but she, like the other guinea pigs, didn't notice or did not care.

Then the guy on his left got it wrong too. "C."

What's going on here?

Then the girl on his left got it wrong. Natalia looked again at Jill and the others. They seemed oblivious to what was happening.

"C."

Then the next guy and the other girl got it wrong, too.

It's plain as day. Momma Bear, line. B.

"C."
"C."

It was Natalia's turn last. She looked from the lines to Jill to the other subjects and back to the lines. It was still obvious that the correct answer was B.

Something is not right.

"It's B," she said cautiously, feeling a little guilty at spoiling everyone else's fun with Jill. She looked at the others, who didn't notice or did not care that she contradicted their answers.

Zombie guinea pigs.

Unfazed, Jill pointed to Natalia and repeated the script for a new set of lines. "Which of lines marked A, B, and C is the same length as this line? We'll start with you." And around it went again and again for what seemed like hours. Most of the time, Natalia and her fellow guinea pigs agreed. But sometimes they got it wrong, and when one got it wrong, the others did too.

They're not guinea pigs, they're sheep.

But Natalia gave the correct answer every time. She might have joined their little joke on Jill, if they had let her in on it.

Just when it seemed she would die of boredom, Jill said, "That concludes our study." As the others stood and started to leave, Jill looked at Natalia and said, "Please stay so that Nathan Sutton, our lead research associate, can debrief you and answer your questions."

As the zombie guinea pigs left, Natalia heard one mumble, "This is the worst job ever."

Nathan soon entered through the same door Jill had. He was carrying a clipboard and he stood beside the blank monitor and smiled at Natalia. Natalia smiled back. He thanked Jill, who let her hair down and took off the glasses and lab coat as she left.

As if reading from a script, Nathan said, "Hi, I am Nathan Sutton, lead research associate. In this debriefing, I will explain more about the study and answer any questions you may have."

Natalia said, "Just one question – what was that? Who were the guinea pig sheep zombies?"

"That's two questions."

"Two questions, then."

"What was that?" he repeated. "That was a trial in a study about conformity. It was not about visual discrimination. Yes, you were misled."

Natalia's eyes widened as she began to understand the setup.

"We are interested in the factors that influence people's decisions to conform to the opinions of a group. The other subjects were actors. They're called confederates – research assistants playing a role."

It makes sense now.

"So you lied," she said, trying to look offended.

"We call it deception," Nathan said as he moved a chair and sat across from Natalia. "The real purpose of the experiment was to learn about peer pressure and conformity. We wanted to find out if you would give the wrong answer in order to conform to the group. It was necessary for us to deceive you to see how you would in react in a real situation in which you were under pressure to conform. You didn't conform. Why not?"

"Well," she started, "it wasn't very realistic. It was obvious that something was not right. Those confederate actors need to loosen up. I thought that maybe it was some kind of joke on poor Jill. I wondered if I should join the joke and give wrong answers, but I didn't feel peer pressure to conform." She paused. "Even if I did, I don't think I would have given in."

"So you weren't fooled," Nathan said. "May I ask a couple of questions about situations in which you really did feel pressure to conform?" he asked, looking at his clipboard.

"Yes."

"Can you recall a situation in your life in which you felt pressure to go along with the opinion or behavior of others, but you did not?"

Every day of high school.

"Not really," Natalia said. "I was always taught that I shouldn't worry about what other people do or what they think of me."

Natalia had felt awkward and ugly for a time during high school. She did care about the opinion of others, and sometimes worried about what people thought of her. She had hated being homeschooled and wearing long jumpers and she had hated her hair and that she was taller than the boys her age.

"Mr. Allen, a man from back home, told me one time, 'Natty Rose, with God as your authority, human opinion is irrelevant.'" She paused and looked into his eyes for a reaction.

Nathan checked his clipboard. "Would you say your religious beliefs are the most important factor in terms of resisting pressure to conform?"

And my parents.

"Yes. I'm a Christian. Being a Christian means standing out sometimes," she said, still watching his eyes. "And, like I said, I was homeschooled. I'm used to being different."

What does he think of me now?

Nathan nodded. "I'm not surprised."

Natalia scowled.

"Not the being a Christian part," he said quickly. "I'm not surprised you didn't conform in the study. You seem like a confident woman – not someone who is easily swayed."

A confident woman. WOMAN. Wow.

"Truth is," he continued, "we are having a hard time replicating the original results. Back in the 1950s, almost everybody – 80% of students like you –

conformed and gave the wrong answer. We think that maybe the Internet or something has made people today more skeptical and harder to deceive."

Natalia had been called a young woman, but never just a "woman." She sat up straight.

"Two more questions," he continued. "Can you recall a situation in your life in which you felt pressure to change your opinion or behavior in order to fit in, and you did?"

Who? Little Miss Goody Two Shoes?

"You mean, a time I gave in to peer pressure?" She searched her memory for an example.

"Yes," he said.

"When I was little, I was in this Bible club and all the kids memorized verses. Most of the kids needed lots of help reciting their verse. Sometimes I would act like I needed help when I really didn't."

Such a nerd. Now I'll have to find another job.

He finally looked away and made a mark on his paper. "Last question. Did you decide about the research assistant job?"

Hooray!

She asked, "Do I get to wear a white lab coat and glasses?"

Nathan laughed. "No, lab coats and glasses scare the babies and make them cry. Rule number one in the baby lab is to never make the babies cry."

He's cute.

"Okay. I'll still take the job," she said, "even without the lab coat. When do I start?"

"Good. You can start next Thursday at 4 o'clock – Room 136, just down the hall. See you then?"

"Yes," said Natalia as she got up to leave. "See you then." She checked her phone and noticed a missed call from her mom.

Chapter 8

As she strolled across campus towards her dorm, Natalia made a mental note to call her mom later. The last remaining sunlight filtered through the leaves, and the street lamps flickered to life. It made the Quad seem magical. When her mom called again – twice in ten minutes – Natalia answered.

"Hi, Mom."

"Hi, Natalia."

Uh-oh, she thought. *She called me Natalia.*

When her mom called her Natty or Natty Rose or dear, Natalia knew everything was okay. When her mom called her by her full name, Natalia Rose Sanders, she knew she was in trouble. When her mom called her Natalia, it usually meant bad news.

Natalia asked, "Is everything okay, Mom?"

"We're fine," her mom said, "but I thought you would want to know that Mr. Allen from church died last night."

"Oh no. I was just telling someone about Mr. Allen. I'm so sorry to hear that, Mom. He was nice."

Natalia meant it. Mr. Allen had been a deacon at First Baptist, but Natalia remembered him from AWANA club. When Natalia was a 4-year-old Cubby, Mr. Allen had helped in her room. He was not scary looking like lots of the men at church, and he did not mind getting on the floor to play. Mr. Allen did not look down his nose on children's activities like many of the deacons. When Natalia was in middle school, Mr. Allen had stopped working with the Cubbies; his knees were bad and it was hard for him to get down on the floor to play. He had switched to serving snacks, driving the church bus, and leading the games for the older kids, so Natalia had still been able to see him. He had been the first person to tell Natalia that she would make a good teacher. He had not had children of his own, but she always thought he would have been a good dad. The last thing Mr. Allen had said as he hugged her goodbye was, "I'm looking forward to hearing all about college when you come home for fall break. I'm praying for you, Natty Rose."

I was looking forward to telling him about it.

"When is visitation?" Natalia asked.

"It's tomorrow evening," her mom answered, "I'm making a nice chicken and rice casserole for the family."

"Would you pay my respects to Mrs. Allen?" Natalia asked.

"I will. I'm going to swing by the funeral home while your brother is at soccer practice."

"Thanks for calling, Mom."

"I love you. I'm praying for you."

"I love you too, Mom. Oh! I almost forgot. I took the job as the research assistant. It doesn't pay much, but it's working with babies and puppets. I start next week."

Natalia thought about Mr. Allen as she brushed her teeth and got ready for bed. He always told the kids at church, "Don't forget to B and P – to brush and potty." It was his way of teaching little children to remember the basics. "You don't forget to brush your teeth and go to the potty, do you? Well don't forget the Bible and prayer. B and P."

When Natalia turned off the bathroom light, the light from Gladys' room peeked under the door. She knocked on Gladys' door and said, "Goodnight, Gladys."

Gladys called back in a singsong voice, "Come in, Natty Rose."

As she opened the door to Gladys' room, she noticed an unusual smell – like sweet burnt popcorn. Natalia was naïve, but not stupid, and she knew immediately that Gladys was stoned. Gladys sat on her bed holding what looked like an oversized fountain pen.

"It's a vaporizer. There's no smell," said Gladys with far away glassy eyes and a silly, crooked smile.

Oh my goodness!

"Want some?" Gladys offered.

"No! I do not want some! I-I-I," Natalia stammered as her mind raced.

My suitemate is a stoner. I'm breathing second-hand smoke. What do I do? I wonder what it's like. Should I tell on her?

"No, I don't want some and I don't want you doing that anywhere near my room!"

Gladys shrugged. "Suit yourself. I'm going out. Lots of parties this weekend. Want to come?"

"No!"

Natalia spun around and ran back to her room, stopping only to lock her bathroom door. She jumped into bed and pulled the covers over her head, just like when she was little and she did not know what else to do. As far as she knew, Natalia had never met someone who used marijuana. She heard once that some friends from the soccer team got some beer one time – but pot, no way.

Drugs. Marijuana. Right next door.

It was quiet in Laurel Dorm. Most of the girls were home for the weekend or at one of the many pre-game parties that night. Natalia decided to call Rachel.

Rachel was her first friend, her best friend, and sometimes it seemed her only friend. Natalia's earliest memories included Rachel. Their families were neighbors and their mothers were pregnant at the same time. From the time they were infants until recently, Natalia and Rachel had always been together. They were more like sisters or cousins than neighbors. When they would argue, Rachel's mom would say, "You girls were best friends since before you were born. Remember that, and now say you're sorry!"

I miss Rachel.

Rachel was a counseling major at Temple Bible College. Natalia knew from personal experience that she would make a good counselor.

She'll know what I should do.

Whenever she was anxious or excited or scared or sad or she did not know what to do, Natalia talked to

Rachel. She looked forward to a good long talk about Gladys and college life so far, but Rachel seemed distracted on the phone. They chatted about classes and cafeteria food.

When Natalia told Rachel about the marijuana she said, "Don't make a big deal out of it. After all, it's legal in like 30 states."

Don't make a big deal?

Natalia asked, "Are you busy? Should I call later?"

"I've got news!" she squealed. Natalia knew that when Rachel squealed it meant she had something exciting to tell.

"I can't talk long because," she paused, "I've got a date." She sang the word 'date.'

"His name is Luke. He's so cute. And nice. I can't wait for you to meet him over fall break."

Natalia was speechless.

Rachel is dating?

"I know it's surprising. I met him in Bible study and we started out just getting together to pray about things. Before long, we were spending lots of time together. I am not ready to get married and neither is

Luke, but we have a real connection. He may be the one. I think it's God's will."

"I'm happy for you, Rachel," Natalia said, but she felt lonely and a little bit jealous. "Have fun on your date."

"I will," Rachel promised. "I will call later and tell you all about him."

Natalia got in bed and pulled the covers over her head. She tried to fall asleep but her mind raced with images of Rachel – married, a Bible college dropout, with two kids and a minivan. She did not think she would like Luke. She imagined the police knocking down the door to arrest Gladys and she worried that they would arrest her, too, for not telling. She thought about Nathan and how cute he must have been with short hair and a military academy uniform.

She knew she had finally fallen asleep when she woke to loud noises coming from the bathroom. Gladys was back. The bathroom light was bright under the door and it made Natalia's room look like the sun was coming up. But it was 2:15am and it sounded like Gladys was cleaning the toilet. Natalia pulled the covers over her head and listened. By 2:18am, it was quiet again. When she peeked from under the covers, the light from the bathroom was still shining under the door.

"Good grief. I can't sleep with that light on," she grumbled.

Natalia tossed off the covers, put on her robe, and stood and listened outside the door.

If she locked me out, I'm going to be mad.

The bathroom door was not locked. Light filled Natalia's room as she slowly pulled it open. The door to Gladys' room was open too and the light in her room was on. Natalia saw her, face down on top of her bed. Natalia thought about just turning off the light and closing the door and going back to bed.

Is she still breathing?

"Gladys? Gladys, are you all right?" Natalia whispered. "Gladys! Are you okay?" She said a little louder.

Gladys did not move. Natalia tiptoed across the room to make sure she was breathing. Gladys smelled like a campfire and cough syrup.

Natalia shook her gently. "Gladys. Do you want take your shoes off and get IN the bed?"

Gladys stirred, but didn't open her eyes. She said, "When I'm high, I don't hear them anymore."

Natalia took a step back.

Hear who? she wondered.

No longer trying to be quiet, Natalia said, "You are drunk, young lady. Come on, let's get you in bed."

'Young lady' was what her mom and dad called Natalia when she was in trouble, but they had never said it because she came in drunk at 2:15am.

"I can't believe you!" She said as she pulled off Gladys' boots. "Are you some kind of alcoholic? What were you thinking, young lady?"

She removed Gladys' jacket and pulled down the bedcovers while Gladys' lay there, mumbling.

"You're underage, young lady. Someone could have taken advantage of you," she said as she rolled Gladys onto her side, put a pillow under her head, and covered her with a blanket.

"Don't come crying to me in the morning when you have a hangover, young lady," Natalia warned her unresponsive suitemate as she turned off the light.

What did she mean by, "When I'm high, I don't hear them anymore?"

Chapter 9

Natalia was already dressed and ready for church Sunday morning when her mom called. She had not slept well; Gladys had come in at 2:00am, making noise and leaving the light on – again.

"Good morning, Mom," she whispered.

"Good morning, Natty Rose," her mom whispered back. "Why are we whispering?"

"My suitemate, Gladys – she was out late last night. I don't want to wake her. I'm worried about her, Mom, and I don't know what to do," said Natalia. "Two nights in a row she's come in drunk." She thought it best not to tell her mom about the marijuana.

"When I met her she looked like a troubled girl. I'll pray for her and put her on the prayer chain at church," her mom promised.

"Thanks, Mom." Natalia appreciated the prayer chain; she had heard the stories of answered prayers – prayers for healing, relationships, wisdom, and protection. She made a mental note to ask the Sunday school class to pray for Gladys, too.

Box will know what I should do.

"I'm going to check on her before I go to church. I'll talk to you later. Bye, Mom."

Natalia tapped on Gladys' door and said softly, "Gladys. Gladys?" She didn't answer, but it was obvious that she was not dead. Her snoring reminded Natalia of the creaky stairs to the basement at home.

Natalia slowly opened the door. There was Gladys, on top of the blanket, still wearing her boots and leather jacket. Natalia looked around the room. It seemed empty. It looked like Gladys' clothes were still in the duffel bag at the foot of the bed. Most girls on the hall, like Natalia, had decorated their rooms with photos and other remembrances of home. Gladys' walls were empty save for one photo stuck to the wall with a thumbtack. Natalia took a closer look. It was an old Polaroid of a young, tall, blonde woman on a stage. She was wearing a bikini and a garter belt, and she had one leg wrapped around a tall pole.

That's Gladys' mom!

Natalia remembered meeting Gladys' mom on move-in day. She had worn a scoop-neck, tight, white tank top, faded jeans, and leather boots with spiked heels. She was very tan and fit.

"Hoochie coochie girl," her dad had said in a whisper.

Natalia's brother had stared, which had earned him a slap on the head from his mom.

Later, as the pews filled at Calvary Way, Natalia felt relieved that she hadn't said something like, "So Gladys, my mom makes casseroles all day and serves on church committees and stuff. What does your mom do?" She wondered what it was like having a mom who was a stripper.

What would they talk about? How was work at the strip club, Mom?

The choir filed in and began to sing; Natalia could see Box, in the back row, smiling ear-to-ear, swaying and clapping and singing *Oh Happy Day*. Joy radiated from his face. The next thing Natalia knew, she was smiling and swaying and clapping, too, and not thinking about Gladys at all. It felt good.

The sermon that morning was about alcohol. Evil alcohol was a regular topic for Pastor Blackmore back home. His message was clear. There should be an 11th commandment – "Thou Shalt Not Drink Alcohol. Period." Jesus may have turned the water into wine, but He sure didn't drink any, and besides, it was just grape juice. At Calvary Way, however, the message was a little different. Their 11th commandment, if a command at all, would have read, "Thou Shalt Not Get Drunk on Alcohol and Let It Come Between You and Christ."

Alcohol was not a part of Natalia's life. She didn't drink, but it did not matter to her if people wanted to. However, she knew alcohol was a touchy subject between Christians, and that sometimes beliefs about alcohol caused division. She remembered the scandal when Mr. and Mrs. Scott had been seen drinking wine at a restaurant in Pineville. The rumor was that some of the deacons had suggested the Scotts go to church somewhere else – so they did.

After the service, Natalia made her way to the College and Career Sunday school classroom. Box was there, out of his choir robe, talking with a tall woman. He smiled and turned toward Natalia.

"Elizabeth, this is Natalia Sanders," he said. "Natalia is a student at State U."

Natalia thought the tall woman must be the pastor's wife or a visiting missionary.

Perfect blonde hair. Subtle but classy jewelry. Wise sparkling eyes.

"Natalia, this is Elizabeth Weber."

Weber?

"Hello. Nice to meet you," the tall woman said.

"Nice to meet you," Natalia answered.

She wondered if Elizabeth Weber was Dr. Weber's wife.

Nah. Weber is a common name.

"I love your blouse."

"Oh, thank you. My mother bought it for me," said Natalia.

"Elizabeth and I are in the choir together," said Box. "We were just talking about how much fun it was singing that song."

"I loved it," said Natalia. "I almost danced!"

Box laughed. Natalia loved the sound.

"I'd better go to my class," said Elizabeth. "See you later, Henry. I will pray about it. Nice to meet you Natalia. I'm praying for you, Henry."

"I'm praying for you, too, Elizabeth," he said as she walked away.

There was plenty for the College and Career Sunday school class to pray about that morning. Box explained again that sharing each other's burdens in prayer was the most important thing they could do. "Praying together is more important than hanging out and eating donuts and drinking coffee, and it is a lot more important than any lesson I could teach. So, what shall we pray about?"

"Pray for a girl in my dorm, she is struggling with an eating disorder," said the first girl.

"Pray for my ex-roommate. He's into internet porn."

"Pray for my friend from high school, she tried to kill herself."

"Pray for my parents. They called and are getting divorced."

"I'd just like us to pray for the whole gay-marriage thing."

"Somebody I knew in high school found out that I'm a Christian and now they're harassing me on Facebook."

"We should pray for the unborn…"

"…that I pass my Chemistry exam."

"...for my suitemate. She is drinking and doing drugs. And I don't think she had a very good home life."

Box did not write anything down, but he remembered every request. Natalia was not comfortable praying aloud for very long, but Box was. It was like listening to one side of a two-sided, intimate conversation.

"Father, I ask your will for Clarissa and her parents. Yes, Lord, you know that her parents are thinking about getting a divorce. Yes, Lord, what you have joined together, let not man put asunder..."

It gave her chills.

After he said "Amen," Box announced that he had a question. As the students moved around for more coffee and donuts, he asked, "If you wanted to build a mini society that made it as difficult as possible for young adults to hold onto their Christian beliefs, what would you build?"

When no one answered, he repeated the question. "What would a society, designed to make it hard to be a Christian, look like?"

"It would be permissive," said the guy with the ex-roommate into porn.

"Right," Box said. "You would build a permissive society in which casual sex and drinking and drugs were normal. What else?"

"It would be a society that said there was no God,' said the girl struggling with chemistry.

"Right again," Box said. "You would make it a society where, if you believe that in the beginning God created the heavens and the earth, you would be subjected to scorn and ridicule, or worse. You would build a society where sin was a meaningless concept – where self-esteem and tolerance were the highest values. You would build a society where morality was relative, flexible, and personal." He shook his head and said, "If you went looking for a place where it was hard to be a Christian, you couldn't do much better than State U., could you?"

Box would make a good professor.

Natalia's mom had made the same points in her own way, before she gave up. Natalia had told her, "I'm not going to State University to drink and have sex and walk away from my faith, Mom! I'm going so I can get the best education and the best teaching job someday. I know you're worried, Mom, but you don't need to be. You raised me right. I've got this."

That was true, but it wasn't that simple. Natalia did not like the unstated expectation that she should get married soon after she started dating, and start having children shortly thereafter. She wanted to do things and ask questions and think for herself. Even though she thought that her parents and the members of First Baptist were a little strict and narrow-minded about some things, she had no plans to rebel. But she did look forward to a measure of freedom, without someone watching and judging her every move.

Box continued, as if he had read her mind. "None of you came here planning to drink and fornicate and walk away from your faith. But how do you make sure it doesn't happen? How do you find your way without compromising? How do you stay in love with God with all your heart, soul, mind, and strength while you are at State U.?"

The girl who asked for prayer for her divorcing parents said, "You keep doing the things you did before, the things that brought you here."

"Yes," said Box. "You find a Bible believing church," he gave a wide, sly smile, "a church with an awesome choir in sweet purple robes." He laughed heartily. "You stay in church."

Still in church. Check.

"You stay in church and you stay in the Word," Box continued. "You keep reading your Bible. How many of you have kept up your pattern of reading the Bible and praying and spending quiet time alone with God?"

Not so much.

"To stay Christian in college, you stay in church, read the Word, pray, and – here's the hard one – you share the reason for your hope. You talk about Jesus and tell others about Him." Box paused. "How many of you have stuffed it?"

He paused and searched their faces.

"You know what I mean. How many of you have had a chance to say something about Jesus but you didn't? Maybe you were afraid of rejection, you thought you didn't know enough, or you were afraid that it would ruin a relationship. I understand that it isn't easy to talk about Jesus at State U."

Strike two.

"You stay Christian in college by refusing to compromise the truth. Every student shows up at college looking for truth. I tell every student I meet – everyone who will listen – that Jesus is *the* Truth, with a capital T. That means you don't have to compromise while you are here, you don't have to leave your faith behind when you walk through the Arch."

Or around it.

After Sunday school, Natalia took the long way back to the dorm, by way of the Quad. She thought about Box's advice. By his standards, she was not off to a good start staying Christian – but she wasn't worried.

I've got this.

She was not the only one drawn to the Quad that afternoon by the clear blue sky and unseasonable warmth. The grass was dotted with students – alone or in small groups. Some were reading. Others were talking or tossing the Frisbee or kicking around a soccer ball. She thought about joining the group playing soccer.

Hi, my name is Natalia, can I play too? Oh, by the way, do you know Jesus?

Instead, she went to her bench to sit and watch the people and to get some sun on her face. She noticed, in the middle of the Quad, where the sun shined through the trees, some girls had stripped down to very little clothing and were working on their late season tans.

Hi, my name is Natalia. Don't you know you're being immodest?

She thought it was no accident that the Frisbee players' bad throws and missed catches usually landed near the sunbathers.

Natalia glanced at her body. She was self-conscious about it. It was not that she thought herself fat or ugly or even out of shape. She was self-conscious because of the catcalls and whistles and double takes and stares and the boys who stared at her chest when she was talking. She was self-conscious because, as long as she could remember, she had been taught the importance of modesty.

"Do not cause your brother to stumble." "Modest is hottest." She had heard it all, over and over again. It was why Natalia usually wore jeans and layers and why her cleavage or belly button had never seen the sunshine at the beach. When she was fifteen, she had gone shopping with Rachel and bought a used dress at a consignment shop. It was a gray mini dress with a scoop neck. She had planned to wear it to church, but so as to be modest, she had worn it with leggings and a white camisole. She had thought it made her look pretty.

The first thing her mom had said when Natalia came downstairs was, "I thought you were getting dressed for church." Natalia had been stunned. As tears started to well up, she had said "I am dressed, Mama."

"Natalia Rose Sanders, you are not properly dressed for church. Young lady, that is a shirt, not a dress. And don't you know what leggings make boys think? How could you even think about wearing that... that... DRESS in the first place? It is immodest. Tell her!" she had said to her husband as she huffed and crossed her arms.

Natalia had felt humiliated and angry.

Her dad had said, "Honey, you don't want to look like a hoochie coochie girl, do you?"

Natalia had wanted to scream, *It's not my problem what boys think about leggings. I love this dress. It makes me look pretty and I'm wearing it!* But she had not. She had said, "No sir, I don't want to look like a hoochie coochie girl." She had gone to her room and stomped around. Then she had changed clothes.

Natalia felt different – out of place on the Quad. She was used to feeling different, she was a homeschooler, but she did not like it. She looked down at her polyester blouse with every button buttoned over a cotton camisole and padded sports bra, and then she looked around at the other girls in their short shorts and tank tops.

She decided to unbutton the top button.

Sunshine is good for me.

Then she unbuttoned the second button, and then she took off her blouse.

I'm still covered, she told herself. The sun and light breeze felt good.

No big deal.

Even if she had taken off her camisole, she would have shown less skin than most of the girls on the Quad. She tilted her face toward the sun, closed her eyes, and felt pretty. She had not been there long when she heard a Frisbee land on the sidewalk nearby. She opened her eyes to see some guy looking her way as he picked it up. He smiled at Natalia and said, "Nice." She put her blouse back on and walked back to her dorm.

When she arrived, Gladys was there. She was awake and sitting on the edge of her bed. Her head was down and her hair covered her face.

Natalia asked, "How are you doing, Gladys?"

"Fine," she answered, without looking up.

"Gladys, how would you like to go to church with me next Sunday?"

Gladys raised her head and looked toward Natalia, but seemed to be looking through her.

Gladys answered, "Why would I do that? All of you Christians are all intolerant, hateful bigots. You hate science, persecute gays, want to control my body, and destroy the environment, too."

Get me out of here.

"Oh. Okay. Never mind." Natalia replied as she walked backwards to her room. "I'm just going to close the door and study now."

Chapter 10

Dr. Weber quietly entered the E. G. Boring Psychology Auditorium at 9:05am. He stood at the lectern and took a deep breath. He was nursing a hangover.

Every Sunday – she goes to church, Sunday school, church again, choir practice, and then back again for night church, he complained to himself.

He opened his tablet to his notes and then clutched the lectern as he began.

"In our last class, we examined the ideas of two giants in the history of science, Charles Darwin and Francis Crick. Today we will look at the contributions of two giants in the history of psychology, Sigmund Freud and Burrhus Frederick Skinner – better known as B. F. Skinner."

And Wednesday night prayer meeting and more choir practice.

When his wife had told him that she believed in Jesus, Ernst Weber was shaken.

She had said, "I know this must be hard for you to understand, Ernst, but it's true. Christianity is true. Jesus is who He said He was."

He had heard her words, but they did not make sense.

"...A personal relationship...Lord of my life... Getting baptized..."

He could not understand how, after 30 years, she could spit in the face of everything he stood for – everything she stood for! It was a cruel joke, a slap in the face. He had hoped it would pass, like some kind of midlife crisis.

Maybe it's because we never had children. He grasped for a logical explanation.

She had tried to explain. "Ernst," she had said, "I love you and I know how hard this is for you. But you know me."

I thought I knew you.

"I was arrogant and full of pride. I never looked at the evidence – for myself."

Maybe a brain tumor?

"I talked to Henry. He gave me some verses to read from the Bible."

Henry Brown. Ha! The Bible, Hrmph!

"When I prayed, Jesus proved himself to me."

Dr. Weber had felt like crying.

"Sigmund Freud was to psychology and psychiatry as Charles Darwin was to biology," he continued for the class. "Freud drew inspiration from Darwin, and he understood the significance of the theory of evolution by natural selection. We go through life believing that our behavior is a series of rational, logical, free-will choices. But Freud showed us that that was an illusion."

Elizabeth Weber's faith had not passed. It had grown. She had started going to church and Sunday school, and she had joined the choir. When she had first told him, "I'm praying for you, Ernst," his sadness had changed to anger and he had started to drink.

"Freud showed us that instead of exercising free will, we are driven by irrational and largely unconscious forces. Freud called the most basic of those forces Id. Id is primitive and seeks pleasure above all else. Id is our inherited human nature. Id contains our basic instinctual drives and propels us to strive to survive and reproduce. Id drives us to seek immediate gratification, to crave sex, to be greedy and steal, and if necessary, to be violent and even kill. Id knows no morals."

That gardener stole my wife.

"Freud described a second part of the mind called ego, from the Latin word meaning 'I'. Ego acts as a mediator between id and reality. Ego contains our conscious awareness and provides reason, judgment, common sense, control, and planning. Ego tries to please id in realistic ways and gives us a way to delay immediate gratification and function in the real world."

I wish he was dead.

"Finally, superego internalizes the rules and cultural norms taught by parents and educators and role models. It strives for perfection and is what we commonly call the conscience. Superego provides our sense of right and wrong, punishes our misbehaviors with feelings of guilt, and allows us to live together in socially acceptable ways."

I should have taken the job at the factory and never brought Elizabeth here. Then she would have never met that gardener, Henry Brown.

Ernst Weber had met his wife while he was in graduate school. He had never seen eyes like hers before. The first time he had seen her, he had known that she would be his wife. Elizabeth Burkhalter had worked at Sutton Manufacturing, an electric motor manufacturer in Leipzig, Germany. The owner of the plant, Nathan Sutton Sr., had commissioned the university to conduct a behavior analysis study to discover the effects of light, temperature, and noise levels on worker productivity. As the lead researcher, Ernst Weber had spent almost a year at the plant.

At first, Elizabeth had resisted his advances. She had been working her way through law school and had been busy with night classes, and studying. But he had been persistent.

The changes Weber had recommended increased productivity at the plant, and Mr. Sutton had been able to build more plants and become very rich. He had offered Weber a job as Vice President of

Production, with a salary forty times his stipend in graduate school. Elizabeth had encouraged him to take the job, but his mind had been made up.

I was destined to make great scientific discoveries.

Elizabeth had agreed to go with him to America for his post-doctoral fellowship, and she had stayed with him when he became an associate professor at State University.

We were happy.

When Mr. Sutton had called, after 30 years, it had taken Dr. Weber by surprise. Mr. Sutton had offered to make a large contribution to the psychology department – large enough to ensure that Dr. Weber's research would never want for money. Dr. Weber had been happy to pull a few strings and get Nathan Jr. into the program.

Money talks.

"My old friend and colleague, B. F. Skinner," Dr. Weber continued, "was the most eminent psychologist of the twentieth century. Where Freud posited that irrational and unconscious forces drive human behavior, Skinner said it was the environment. We are born blank slates with no innate knowledge. Skinner showed that there was no real human nature, and that to understand human behavior it was unnecessary to point to internal mental states like consciousness, emotions, intuition, and free will."

I should have spent more time with her when her mother died.

"We have a deep-seated drive to survive, to seek pleasure, and to avoid pain."

He thought about calling his wife. He would tell her he understood how much she missed her mother. He would tell her he was sorry he had not spent more time with her when she needed him. He would tell her that he understood how much she wanted to see her mother again someday. He would be more sensitive to her feelings and he wouldn't tell her any more to get over it. He would tell her that he loved her and needed her and that he did not want to lose her. He would tell her that he would try to understand and accept her religion.

But he knew he couldn't say those things. He knew he would probably just get mad and start to cry. He did that a lot, lately.

"Skinner believed that there were no interesting differences between species. Humans, primates, and labs rat differ only in terms of the stimuli they can perceive and their repertoire of responses."

After class, as he walked back to his office, Dr. Weber thought about Freud and Skinner, rewards and reinforcement, emotions and free will, and Elizabeth and that damn gardener.

Skinner was full of it.

He saw the Cowboy, Jessie, preaching under the Arch. During the lawsuit, Elizabeth had called him an imbecile and an embarrassment.

Now she is one of them.

Chapter 11

Room 136 in James Hall looked more like a nursery than a classroom. The floor had carpet and the walls were painted in bright colors; instead of moldy desks and a chalkboard, the room was furnished with stuffed animals, rocking chairs, and a changing table.

"The purpose of this study is to understand baby morality," Nathan explained to his two new research assistants. "We use puppet shows to learn about babies' moral decision-making.

"Your job, Matt, is to greet the moms when they arrive and make them and their babies feel comfortable. Review the informed consent forms and be sure to get a signature here and here, and to get initials here and here and there."

Moms will trust that face, Nathan thought. He had selected Matt as a research assistant because of his dark eyes and square jaw. Matt appeared wise and authoritative, which Nathan hoped would help assure the mothers that their babies would be safe.

And keep them from asking a lot of unnecessary questions, he thought.

Nathan loved research, but it was difficult. There was so much paperwork, especially when doing experiments with young children. It was difficult to find enough mothers willing to give up an hour for a

$20 stipend. It was difficult too, because if a baby got startled or scared or would not stop crying, they still had to pay the stipend. He needed lots of alert and happy babies.

The advancement of science takes money.

Nathan believed he was on the brink of discovering something important in the basement of James Hall, something that he was sure would revolutionize the way psychologists understood morality. He had learned in his undergraduate classes that psychologists from Freud to Piaget to Kohlberg believed that humans began life as amoral, little, thoughtless blobs. Parents, society, and religion teach the blobs to behave morally, to experience guilt and shame and empathy; but Nathan Sutton would show that it was not that simple.

Technically, the baby morality study was Dr. Weber's research. Dr. Weber was the department head and his name would be listed first when the research was published. It did not matter that Weber was disrespectful and rude to him – Nathan's name would be there and he would be a published scientist. It would be a feather in his cap to have his name on such important work. He would probably become famous in developmental psychology circles.

I'll finally get a following on Twitter.

Weber rarely came to the basement of the Psychology department. Nathan was in charge.

Nathan had supervised the remodeling of the classroom, had designed and built the miniature black box theater for the puppet shows, had selected the research assistants, and had collaborated with the local childcare centers and preschools to recruit babies.

"Natalia, your job is to make the babies feel comfortable. Play with them while mom does the paperwork. Then bring them both through this door."

He opened a door and led Natalia into the adjoining room, leaving Matt behind. Nathan turned and playfully wagged his index finger. He said, "and remember, no crying babies."

"Are you ready to learn the show?" he asked as he turned to open the door to the adjoining room.

"Yes," she answered.

"What kind of puppeteering have you done?"

"We had a puppet ministry at church. Every summer we had backyard Bible camp and vacation Bible school. We made puppets and props, we wrote scripts, had rehearsals, and made flyers to hang around town. The idea was we would teach kids about Jesus with puppets. Mostly it kept the kids busy while the adults had prayer meeting."

"You *are* over qualified," he laughed. "Come back stage and I'll teach you the moves."

He led Natalia behind the tiny stage through a black curtain. "I haven't found a three-handed research assistant, so it takes two people."

"There isn't much room," Natalia observed.

Nathan did not respond. He knew that anybody could wear a floppy-eared bunny hand puppet and roll balls around. It was because of the close quarters that he was selective choosing his puppet assistant.

We'll be working very close together...

There was a small bench where Nathan and Natalia would sit. "You sit on that side."

I'll show you the moves.

Their shoulders touched. She tucked her hair behind her ear and looked at him and smiled, but did not move away.

"Here's how it works. The curtain goes up and there are three puppets – one in the middle and one on each side. You can see that they're all different colors. The story is simple: the middle puppet wants to play with a ball. The puppet on the right plays nice and rolls the ball back. You're the nice puppet. The puppet on the left doesn't roll the ball back. Mean puppet. The

114

mean puppet keeps the ball and runs away and the curtain falls. That's the show."

"That's it?" she asked.

"Yes. Then you get up and take the nice and mean puppets out front to offer the babies a choice – to find out which puppet they prefer. I watch from back here to record whether the baby reaches for the nice or the mean puppet. If they are too young to control their hands enough to reach, we measure which puppet they look at longest." He pointed to a camera concealed behind a stuffed teddy bear. "We can mix it up a little and you can be the mean puppet if you want; we'll change the colors of the nice and mean puppets each time, so we're sure we are not measuring a preference for colors, but otherwise the show is the same every time. If everybody shows up and nobody cries, we perform six times a night."

Natalia put on the blue puppet and asked in a squeaky voice, "Do we have any lines?"

"No lines. You're silly," he said with a smile. "You must mistake this for the theatre department. Let's practice."

It was a good night at the baby lab. It did not happen often that all six mothers and their little ones showed up. And when they did show up, it was mind-numbingly boring to do six shows in a row. But that afternoon, Nathan's mind was not numb. He was alert and interested in Natalia's every move. She smelled good and he liked watching her interact with the babies. Not only did she not make the babies cry, her broad and fresh and sincere smile and her sparking green eyes made the babies and their mothers and Nathan laugh and smile.

Dr. Weber would say she's a high value mate – great skin, full lips, bright eyes, white teeth, and killer figure.

After the last mother had left and Matt was gone, Nathan said, "It is a good day when everyone shows up and nobody cries. You did good work."

"I have a question," Natalia said as she raised her hand beside her face as if to ask for permission to speak. "Do they always choose the nice puppet?"

Nathan laughed. "Not every time, but about 87% of the time they do."

He understood that 87% was a powerful effect. It meant he was onto something big – something inborn in all children, a kind of moral compass. It looked to Nathan like she was about to ask another question.

"Wow," she said instead. "That's a lot."

Nathan laughed again and said, "Listen, on Thursdays me and the other TAs get together at *Papa*

Joe's to hang out and talk about psychology and stuff. You should come sometime."

She asked, "Is that the place downtown across from the Arch?"

"It is," he answered. "On the weekend it's pretty crazy in there, but on Thursdays, not so much. My friend is the bartender and he saves us a table in the back."

"Sounds interesting." She touched her hair and said, "Maybe I will…sometime. Thanks for the job. I had fun. See you later," she said as she spun around and walked out.

Not too fast, Nathan, he cautioned himself as he stuck his head out of room 136 to watch her walk away.

Papa Joe's was a college town pub on Main Street, directly across from The Arch. It was an institution at State University. It was once a gas station and repair garage, but there was more money in beer and pizza, so *Papa Joe's* the Chevron station had become Papa Joes' the pub. They served pizza and wings and sandwiches and there was a good selection of craft beers. The bartender was Nathan's friend. Every Thursday night, Nathan and his team of teaching assistants got together at their usual table in the back to talk and laugh and drink. Nathan always sat at the head of the table, like the chairman of the board, and shared his knowledge and witty humor.

Amy, Jill, Doug, Ande, and Billy Ray were already there when Nathan arrived. They seemed happy to see him.

"Hey, Nathan! Where have you been?"

"We wondered if you were coming."

They liked Nathan. They knew that someday, after he had made a name for himself, they would say that they had known him when.... Technically, they all worked for Dr. Weber, but they rarely saw him. Nathan was their boss. They went to Nathan, not Dr. Weber, when they had questions or needed advice. Dr. Weber approved their research if it fit with his larger objectives, but it was Nathan's job to supervise and make sure it was conducted properly.

"We have a question for you, Nathan," said Jill from the far end of the table as Nathan poured a beer from the pitcher they passed his way. "If we could surgically remove your brain and put it in Doug's head, and replace your brain with Doug's, would you say that you had a new body? Or would Doug say he had a new brain?"

Nathan smiled. "I'd say I got cheated. Have you looked at Doug's body?" They all laughed and

Nathan motioned to the waitress to bring another pitcher of beer.

It looked to the others like Nathan listened attentively as they talked about their respective research projects, but his thoughts were on his new assistant puppeteer.

She touched her hair. She smiled and did not move away. Check, check, and check.

He thought that it might take a little longer, because she was a Christian, but he was sure he would date her.

By fall break.

"What do you think, Nathan? Is it fair?" asked Amy Martinez, bringing him back from his thoughts about Natalia. Amy's research involved conducting surveys to learn more about the evolution of homosexual mate selection. Nathan wondered if Amy was more interested in advancing her personal agenda than advancing science. "Do you think it's fair," she repeated, "that the research on mate selection strategies always focuses on heterosexuals?" She had a whiney, complaining tone. "I understand that we need to understand what guys look for in girls and what girls look for in guys, but strategies for same sex selection must have evolved, too. Isn't that every bit as worthy of study?"

Amy believed that prejudice against LGBTs was everywhere, even among her colleagues who claimed to be open-minded and tolerant. Nathan was not sure he believed people were homosexual by birth. One night at *Papa Joe's,* he had made the mistake of asking Amy how evolution explained homosexuality. "If the genes producing homosexuality aren't passed down because the people with the gene don't reproduce, why wasn't homosexuality selected against long ago?"

"Evolution doesn't care," she had said loudly, "about sexual preferences. All that matters is that the populations thrive. There are plenty of heterosexuals around to replenish the population, as long as everyone else is working cooperatively to provide a supportive environment." She got angrier as she spoke. "The biological imperative isn't to reproduce at all cost, it is to love one another – to cooperate and build communities." She had eventually stormed out and called them all homophobes.

Not wanting to make the same mistake, Nathan changed the subject. "What's the Cowboy up to these days, Ande?"

Ande Phinney's research was about attitudes toward religion and social issues among college students. Her hypothesis was that college students became less accepting of religious dogmatism and became more liberal on social issues. Her team of research assistants went to wherever the Cowboy was preaching and asked people who stopped to listen to complete a survey about religious attitudes. She believed that organized religion – especially the Christian religion – was responsible for many of the world's problems and that people like the Cowboy should be silenced for the greater good.

"He's the same," she answered, "spewing his hateful intolerance. It's hard to find people to survey because not many people stop to listen to him. Now, he recognizes my assistants and tries to convert them. Yesterday, I stopped to check on Lilly – she's one of my new assistants. She wasn't even trying to give surveys. She was sitting beside the Cowboy on the steps by the Arch, just talking to him. When I confronted her, she said, 'But Ande, some of what he says makes sense.' I think I'm going to have to let her go."

Nathan frowned. "We have to be careful. If we fire her because she turns Christian, we could end up with a lawsuit, you know."

"I know," she said. "Don't get me wrong. I understand religion. I know that it was important, when we lived in small hunter/gatherer societies, for everyone to co-operate and contribute and play fair. I understand that watched people are nice people, and that an all-seeing eye in the sky was important to the evolution of culture. I understand that small-minded people like Lilly and the Cowboy need the comforting crutch of belief in an after-life. But it seems like a cruel joke that evolution programmed us to believe in a lie. Like Weber says, 'science made it possible to find real truth.'"

Nathan knew it was time to change the subject again, before Ande got too worked up. Sometimes, when she had too many beers, Ande cried and shouted and pounded the table and talked about her father, the charismatic pastor who fondled Ande and hit her mother.

Nathan refilled his glass and asked, "How's your research, Billy Ray?"

He snarled his lip and answered, "It's disgusting," and everyone laughed. Billy Ray Sweatman was interested in disgust. His research had earned him the nickname 'The Doctor of Disgust.' Billy Ray was studying Weber's theory that disgust evolved as an adaptation, and that morals, especially the taboos, were byproducts of disgust. He seemed to enjoy grossing people out. His job was to show subjects photos of things like blood, feces, injuries, rotted flesh, and prison camps and ask them to rank which was most disgusting.

"We have good data from last semester," Billy Ray said. He had a mouthful of pizza and got sauce in his beard. He chewed as he continued, "This semester we are collecting data around race and sexual orientation."

Didn't your mother teach to not talk with your mouth full?

Billy Ray washed down the pizza with beer and answered, "We show photos of people kissing. The subjects rate the photos on a scale from zero to five. Zero means it is not at all disgusting and five means completely and totally disgusting. We start with plain old different sex, same race kisses – white guys kissing white girls then black guys kissing black girls. All zeros. No disgust."

Nathan wondered if the research was having an effect on Billy Ray.

Billy Ray dipped a bread stick in the sauce and looked at Jill. "Then we move to mixed race different gender kisses. Black guys kissing white girls and visa versa. I shouldn't have been surprised, but I was. Lots of people, I mean lots of the freshmen psychology students in the study, still have issues with mixed race relationships."

Nathan thought it was disgusting the way Billy Ray looked at Jill when he talked about race.

Does he think she doesn't know she's black?

Billy Ray rotated his head to look at Amy and said, "Then we switched to photos of same sex, same race kisses."

Now stare at the gay girl.

Amy interjected, "Let me guess. The same sex kisses are more disgusting than mixed race?"

"No," Billy Ray answered, "not a significant difference. That was a surprise."

He looked at Amy and then at Jill. "It is the photos of same sex, different race kisses that people rate most disgusting. The highest ratings are for the black men kissing white men. One guy quit the study and stormed out."

Amy snorted in disapproval and Jill went to the bathroom.

Nathan said, "You're disgusting sometimes."

"I know." Billy Ray laughed and wiped his mouth with his shirtsleeve. "But think about it. Is feeling disgusted about same sex and opposite race relationships something we learn to feel, or is it programmed like disgust at the sight of rotted flesh?" Billy Ray sucked the meat off a chicken wing as he emphasized the words, "rotted flesh."

"Are we taught to be racist homophobes or are we born that way?" Nathan asked. He took a big drink from his glass. "I know what Weber would say. He would say it was just like religion. We're wired by evolution to be religious, we're wired to be wary of those who don't look like us, and we're wired to be disgusted by homosexuality."

Amy snorted again and said, "But Weber also says science and reason has made it possible to overcome our biases," and she, too, went to the bathroom.

Doug asked, "So Nathan, what's going on with Weber?"

As lead research assistant and lead teaching assistant, Nathan met with Dr. Weber every week. Nathan liked the privilege of access to the great Dr. Ernst Weber, but Nathan knew he was not a happy man. Dr. Weber was getting harsher and angrier and he always seemed distracted. Nathan knew why. He knew that Mrs. Weber was a Christian now and he knew that Dr. Weber was taking it hard.

"I'm not sure," he lied, "maybe problems at home. Did you know," he asked, "that years ago, the Street Preacher was only allowed to preach in one little free speech zone near the student center? He got a lawyer from some Christian legal society and sued. Dr. Weber's wife defended the university."

"I didn't know about that," said Doug. "What happened?"

"She argued that the preacher was engaged in hate speech and that State U. had a right to limit it. She lost."

"I heard she turned Christian and started going to church," said Doug.

"I heard that, too," said Nathan quietly.

Amy and Jill returned from the bathroom. Jill asked, "Anybody going to the game?"

One of their favorite topics was the stupidity of the whole football-crazed culture at State University. Nathan guessed that Jill asked about the game to make it clear that she was not interested in hearing more about Billy Ray's research.

"Can you believe they have to put up little fences around the flower beds on the Quad to keep people from peeing on them – or worse? It's disgusting," laughed Billy Ray, taking the hint.

"I'm going to call it a night," Nathan announced. "Good night, everybody."

"Aww, don't go. It's still early," the others protested.

"Do you want company?" asked Jill. She was not shy about wanting to be more than Nathan's colleague. She made it clear that she was still available.

Been there, done that.

"No. It's tempting," he answered as he finished his beer, "but I'm really tired. I'll see you all on Monday."

Chapter 12

Natalia woke with a start. She had been dreaming she was a cave woman in a leopard-skin tunic; she had been about to be eaten by a saber-toothed tiger, but she could not scream. When she opened her eyes, she saw Gladys on her knees beside the bed, looking at her. Natalia scrambled to sit upright and pulled the blanket up to her chin.

"What are you doing?" she whispered as loud as she could.

"I couldn't sleep. So I came over to see if you were studying or something."

Natalia looked at the clock – it was 3:45am.

"Are you drunk?"

"No. Maybe if I was I could sleep. I was watching you. You were having a nightmare."

This is too creepy, thought Natalia.

"I saw the scar on your lip."

Natalia jerked her hand to her lip. To see the scar Patches gave her when she was three years old, one had to look closely.

Too close.

"I got bitten by a dog one time, too," Gladys said as she showed Natalia a scar on her hand. "Sparkles thought I was stealing his bone."

Natalia did not know what to say. "I'm sorry Sparkles bit you," she said to be polite. She made a mental note to double check the bathroom door from now on. "Next time, would you knock, please?"

"Okay." Gladys shrugged. "I think I'll go write my paper for English Lit."

When Gladys had left, Natalia jumped from her bed and locked the bathroom door. She got back in bed and pulled the blanket over her head. She was shivering; she thought of Gladys' bad breath, pale skin, skinny lips, and bloodshot eyes, staring at her in the dark and getting close enough to see the scar.

How did she know it was a dog?

Natalia got up again to double-check that she had locked the bathroom door. She got back in bed, covered her head again, and wondered which scared her more – the dream or Gladys.

Gladys. Definitely.

She did not sleep much after that. She was awake when her mom called.

"Good morning, Mom, what are you doing?"

"Good morning, Natty Rose. I'm making a casserole for the Romano family. Mrs. Romano's mother died last night."

"Oh. I'm sorry. Did we know her mother?"

"No, she lived in Arizona. But you know what I always say – nothing says we're thinking of you like a good casserole."

"That is what you always say, Mom," Natalia replied, hoping it didn't sound sarcastic.

"How is your new job, Dear?" Natalia's mom asked.

Natalia thought, *There's this cute guy and I think I flirted with him*, but she knew better than to say it.

"It was fun," she answered. "The babies are so cute. I play with them and make them feel comfortable. Then we do the puppet show and I play with them again. It is pretty easy, and the people I work with are nice."

"Your father wants to know if you've met any interesting boys."

Natalia knew that the question was not from her dad. She thought about Nathan's offer to go to *Papa Joe's*.

It would be with a group, so it wouldn't be as a date.

Natalia had never been on a real date. She was not allowed to date. She had been taught all her life that even when she was old enough to date, she still shouldn't. She had been taught that she should not date until she was ready to get married. And when she was ready to receive suitors, they should have a courtship and not really date in a worldly way. She was only allowed to hang out with boys in mixed sex groups. She could go to movies and skating and to Waffle Queen with guys, but always in a group.

No pairing up.

When they were younger, Natalia and Rachel had talked a lot about getting married – not about dating, just getting married. Rachel was not allowed to date either. They had talked for hours and had started each sentence with, "When I get married..." They had played the Married Name Game, which involved trying out their married names if they married one of the cute boys in town. "Mrs. Natalia Watkins." Not good, so Steve Watkins was out as a future husband. Mrs. Natalia North sounded good, so Ralph North had potential.

Mrs. Natalia Sutton?

It had not been a big deal -- not being allowed to date – as there wasn't anyone she had wanted to date back home. The truth was, she was not sure she wanted to get married. Sure, she played games and imagined getting married, but she could not imagine spending the rest of her life with a guy. She could, however, imagine dating Nathan.

"Tell Dad no boyfriend yet, but I'm working on it."

"That's a good one," her mom laughed. "But really, have you met any interesting boys?"

"No, Mom." she said, hoping the irritation in her voice was clear. "I'm meeting guys – 'boys', as you say. The guys I work with, Matt and Nathan, they're nice. But I'm not looking for *interesting* boys. I need to get ready for church, Mom. I'll call you tonight."

"I'm praying for you, Natty Rose."

Natalia selected her gray mini dress and leggings to wear to church. She felt pretty as she walked across campus to Calvary Way.

If my mother could see me now.

Mrs. Weber and Box and the rest of the choir opened worship at Calvary Way that morning with a rocking rendition of Just a Little Talk with Jesus. Natalia loved that song. She smiled and swayed and clapped.

I wish I was a good singer.

During announcements, there was a call for volunteers to work in the AWANA club. The Cubbies performed a cute puppet show and recited verses and sang a song. The club commander said, "All I ask you to do is pray about whether God is leading you to work with these precious little gifts from God."

Natalia's mind was made up about AWANA. There was no need to pray about it. There was no way she was going volunteer. She could not remember a time when she was not in AWANA – except during summer breaks.

I deserve a break.

Her mom and dad had helped start AWANA at First Baptist when Natalia when was four years old – old enough to be a cute Cubbie. Every Wednesday evening, while the adults were in prayer meeting, Natalia had played games, earned awards, made craft projects, and recited the verses she had memorized. When she was sixteen years old, Natalia had earned the Citation award, AWANA's highest honor. She was certain she had memorized more verses than anyone else on her hall, in the whole dorm, and maybe all of State University. If State U. had a sword drill team, Natalia thought, she could be team captain.

Maybe I will help in AWANA when I have kids, she told herself as she walked to Sunday school. Box and Mrs. Weber were in the hall, talking.

She looks upset.

They acknowledged Natalia, but it was clear to her that it was a private conversation.

When they came into the classroom, Box made an announcement. "Some of you already know Elizabeth Weber," he said. "Elizabeth has agreed to teach this class for me when I'm absent." He led a polite applause and said, "We are glad you are with us, Elizabeth, in more ways than one."

Natalia thought Mrs. Weber looked like she was going to cry.

"Thank you, Henry," she said, looking at Box and then the floor.

"Elizabeth agreed to share her personal testimony this morning, after we pray. When you hear about her life as an atheist and how she came to Christ, you'll agree that she is an excellent fit for this class. Now," he continued, "it is time for the main event. How can we pray this week?"

"...Keep praying for the girl in my dorm with the eating disorder. She's still losing weight."

"...Pray for my mom. She has bipolar disorder and we think she's stopped taking her medication. The people at the church she attends don't think it is right to take psychiatric medicines. That makes it harder."

"...Pray for my friend back home. Her father was our pastor and he was forced by the deacons to step down and now she has to move."

"...Keep praying for my parents. They called again and are going to go to counseling to try to work things out."

"... Pray for my suitemate. Her name is Gladys. She's been acting strange. I woke up last night and she was in my room staring at me."

"...Pray for my husband, Ernst. He's having a hard time accepting that I'm a Christian now. And pray that God would touch his heart like He did mine."

She IS Dr. Weber's wife!

Natalia was shocked.

Distinguished atheist Professor Ernst Weber's wife is a Christian.

She almost laughed aloud, but she could tell from Mrs. Weber's face that it was no laughing matter.

There were no more prayer requests, so Box said, "Elizabeth, go ahead and tell us how God touched your heart, and then we will pray for Ernst and for you and these other requests."

Mrs. Weber took a deep breath, sat up straight and tall, and said, "Henry was right when he said I lived a lifetime as an atheist. My parents were atheists and they taught me to be one, too. They were attorneys and I became an attorney like my parents. At first, I was a lukewarm atheist. I did not believe in God, but I did not give it serious thought. It didn't bother me that other people believed. But after my husband and I came here – he wasn't my husband yet, but that is another story – I did legal work for Family Services. I saw terrible things done by religious people. I started to blame religion, and to hate people who believed in God."

She shook her head as if fighting off a bad memory. "I decided that the best thing I could do, as an attorney, was use the law to fight religion, so I did. I was like Saul of Tarsus. I had a few high profile cases, like when I tried to get Jessie – you know, the street preacher – kicked off campus. I tried to get Henry fired for talking about Jesus. But mostly, I threatened people. If faculty or staff talked about God on this campus, and I heard about it, I called them to my office and reminded them that this was a state university and that there was separation of church and state. I wrote letters to religious student groups threatening to have their charters revoked for their intolerance and bigotry."

Mrs. Weber's expression changed. She took another deep breath, smiled, and looked at Box. "But even though I became an aggressive and anti-religious atheist, I still was unsure about why. I never examined the evidence for my disbelief. I was an atheist because my parents were atheists and I just took it for granted. More importantly, even though I persecuted believers, they were praying for me. When the atheist organization, State University's Committee for Reason, invited Henry to a debate, I went. I thought he was a fool. But he stood in front of a room full of seething atheists, including me, and gave the first thorough explanation for belief in God I had ever heard. He explained the fine-tuning of the universe, the moral argument for God, he talked about the evidence for Jesus, and he gave his personal testimony. Then he gave what I know now is called, the invitation. He gave an invitation to a room full of atheists," she laughed.

She looked away, as though deep in thought. "I always assumed that believers had blind faith – faith without evidence. The idea that there was evidence for God and evidence for Jesus intrigued me. I am an attorney, after all. I felt compelled to examine the evidence for myself – to see where it led. Henry helped me. We talked for hours. When we finished talking, he always said, 'I'm praying for you, Elizabeth.' I did not mind. I read the New Testament and everything else Henry recommended."

Box was beaming.

"One day," she said as her smile turned and her lip quivered, "one day, when he said, 'I'm praying for you, Elizabeth,' I looked at him and said, 'I'm ready for you to pray *with* me, Henry.' And he did. I examined the evidence for myself and my verdict was that it was true. We sat on a bench on the Quad and I accepted Christ as my Lord and Savior."

Natalia wiped away a tear. She was not the only one.

It was quiet for a while. Then Box prayed. He thanked God for saving Elizabeth. He prayed for the girl with the eating disorder – that she would see herself like Jesus sees her. He prayed for the mom with bipolar disorder, and he prayed that her church family would support her and not condemn her for taking medications. He prayed for Gladys and her strange behavior, and for everyone else struggling with mental pain and suffering. He prayed for comfort and healing. He prayed for the Church and for pastors and youth leaders and children's workers. He prayed for parents and marriages and families. He prayed for Ernst Weber – that God would touch his heart and open his eyes.

After he prayed, it was very quiet.

Then Box stood and said, "That makes me want to hug people." He laughed and said, "Let's take a break. Hug somebody, get a donut if you want one, then there's something else I want to talk about."

Natalia liked hugs. She got five. She liked donuts, too – cream filled – but she got a bran muffin instead. After a few minutes, Box said over the commotion, "I want to talk about something. Ya'll stop hugging and settle down."

Natalia went back to her seat on a big couch. Box stood beside the girl who asked for prayer for her mother with bipolar disorder.

"Phyllis honey, I'm sorry about your mom. We live in a fallen world – corrupted by sin and death, and that means things go wrong with our bodies and with our brains. Bipolar disorder is difficult – but it is treatable. I know lots of people with bipolar. The thing that makes me angry is the people in that church telling her not to take medicine."

He walked to the front of the room. "If somebody has cancer or needs food and shelter, Christians are right there with aid. No questions asked. But if someone is suffering up here," he pointed to his temple, "we don't want to hear about it. Pray harder, we say. Get rid of that sin we know you're hiding, and whatever you do, don't take medicine." He shook his head. "That's not right."

Natalia thought about Gladys.

"My wife, Michelle, doesn't mind me sharing that she's struggled with depression her whole adult life. She's the godliest, most prayerful woman you will ever meet. But she has a mood disorder and has to take medication. Shoot, I take medications for high sugar, high blood pressure, and high cholesterol. What is the difference? I'm not saying that hidden sin is not a problem. I am not saying prayer isn't important. What I have a problem with is Christians who say that all mental pain and suffering is just the direct result of sin and too little prayer. It's just not that simple."

Natalia thought about what Gladys had said, "When I'm high I don't hear them." She felt intrigued and frightened.

After Sunday school, instead of stopping on the Quad to enjoy the sunshine, Natalia walked straight back to Laurel dorm. Gladys was not there, but her bathroom door was open. Natalia looked inside. She saw that Gladys had finally decorated the walls of her room; but it was not decorated with photos and remembrances of home. Instead, there were dozens of pages ripped from magazines and stuck to the walls with thumbtacks. Natalia knocked on the open door before going in for a closer look.

Gladys' walls were decorated with photographs of girls with red hair.

Redheads?

Natalia felt a chill.

I'm a redhead... Not just creepy. Scary creepy.

She quickly returned to her room, locking the door behind her.

Chapter 13

At 9:12am, Dr. Weber quietly opened the door to the E. G. Boring Psychology Auditorium and poured himself through. He walked, head down, across the stage. The lights in the auditorium seemed brighter than usual.

"Today's lecture is on a topic about which I am sure you are all very interested. Sex."

He had still been asleep on the couch that morning when his wife had left for work. He rarely overslept, but he had been up late drinking wine and thinking about his wife and that damned gardener, Box. He made a mental note to never again take muscle relaxants and drink wine at the same time.

It is all his fault. He thought. *It's his fault. All his fault. Damn him!*

He tapped his tablet and asked, "What was the biggest problem faced by our earliest ancestors? After not being eaten by wild animals, that is. It was sex – same as today. Now, I know that a big part of the college experience is 'hooking up', trying it out, and seeing what works – what you like, and what you don't like."

There were some giggles and nervous glances, especially from the girls.

"But for our ancestors during the Pleistocene Epoch, the stakes were higher. Finding and attracting a suitable mate, having offspring, and raising those offspring to adulthood so that they, in turn, would have more offspring, was crucial to the survival of our species."

His head was throbbing.

"Imagine you are a female living 200,000 years ago. You probably live in small groups of 25 to 50 members. Your group spends much of its time finding food and shelter and safety and raising offspring. You have a limited supply of eggs and if you get pregnant, you must invest great energy, at great risk, to carry the baby for nine months and then raise it to maturity. It is crucial that you select the best possible mate, a mate with good genes who can provide for you and the offspring. Human females, like those of our primate cousins, acquired mate selection strategies, designed by evolution, to maximize the likelihood that their children would survive."

Dr. Weber knew from personal experience that the psychology of gender roles and the evolution of mate selection strategies were hot button topics that made some people angry.

"Those strategies are evident today in modern females' preference for strong, high status males with abundant physical and material resources to provide for them and their offspring. A high value mate then, from the female perspective, was a male who was healthy, stable, dependable, and could provide protection and provision."

Before there was social media, students protested outside of Dr. Weber's classroom and called him a sexist pig and worse for suggesting that women were gold diggers competing for successful wealthy men. Eventually, his critics had switched to social media – mean Facebook posts and tweets. *#WeberIsSexist.*

"The problem, in the Pleistocene Epoch and today, is that every other female in the group is looking for the same qualities in a mate – and the pool of suitable males is limited.

"If you were a male in that same group of early humans, your sexual calculus was different. Females evolved a preference for males who could provide and protect. What was attractive to your male ancestors?"

"A hottie!" shouted someone from the back of the auditorium.

Dr. Weber said, "That's right. And what was hot to our ancient male ancestors? The same characteristics that men find attractive today. Men are attracted to clear skin, full lips, clear eyes, good teeth, large breasts, and the right waist-to-hip ratio. Why? Because those traits are associated with reproductive success. Those traits suggest good health, quality genes, and the ability to produce and raise offspring. Males evolved to prefer these characteristics, and the competition was fiercest for the highest value females. Narrow hips, small breasts, and bad skin, hair, and teeth predicted less reproductive success. There was less competition for females with those traits."

He paused for effect – to let it sink in that evolution sexually objectifies the female body and equates a woman's worth with her body's appearance and sexual function.

"The problem, again, is that every other male in the group is looking for the same qualities. The number of offspring that one healthy female could have was limited. One healthy male, however, could have virtually limitless offspring – but so could every other healthy male. This set up a competition with existential consequences. The competition was to attract and impregnate as many females as possible. The sexual relationship between men and women has been described as a war. This war is rooted in the competing reproductive objectives of males and females. Females compete for good providers and males compete for hotties. This competition is the root of many problems today. Promiscuity, jealousy, infidelity, cuckoldry, and perhaps even rape and sexual violence, are rooted in the struggle to reproduce. Keep in mind, evolution doesn't say what is right. Evolution is amoral."

Sometimes Dr. Weber was accused of using evolution to defend rape and sexual assault. More so than his statements about God, religion, and gender differences in mate selection strategies, his comments about adultery and rape made him a target for criticism from all sides. One time a girl had stood up in class with a sign screaming, "DR. WEBER DEFENDS RAPE."

Pastors and priests had condemned him on several occasions for cheapening the institution of marriage and justifying adultery, but the criticism did not bother him. In fact, he enjoyed it. At least, he used to. His headache was getting worse, so he decided to head it off.

I don't feel like fighting.

"I'm not saying rape is right. I'm not saying cheating on your spouse is right, so don't shout at me or protest outside my office. What I am saying is that human sexual behavior, like everything else, was designed by evolution. But we can and should rise above our evolved predispositions – our temptations, if you will."

Dr. Weber understood temptation. He saw himself as a high value mate. Every semester, one or two co-eds, with all the signs of their health and reproductive value on display, would come to his office with questions about this or that, talking about how much they loved psychology. But it was clear what they

145

really wanted and what they were offering in return. During his first fifteen years at State University, he had resisted the tug of his evolved urges to spread his genes far and wide, until one day he didn't. Then he did it again, and then again. When he was eventually caught sleeping with students, he had almost lost his job. Elizabeth had represented him at the university tribunal. She had gotten him off with a written reprimand. It had been much worse for him at home.

I shouldn't have begged her to stay.

Elizabeth had said she was leaving him. She had rented an apartment and packed her belongings. Dr. Weber had begged her to stay. He had told her that he had only ever loved her, but she had left anyway. While they lived apart, he had courted her, as he had when they met. At first, she had resisted his advances, but he had been persistent. She had finally agreed to take him back on the conditions that he promised never to cheat again and that they get married. He had promised, and they had been married on the Quad.

"So, as you look around the room and think about who you would like to hook up with and who you wouldn't, know that you are actually engaging in a very complex adaptation that evolved over a long period of time to solve problems related to sex. You think you are attracted to certain characteristics in the opposite sex because of personal preferences or your individual understanding of love and beauty. But you are ultimately responding to a program written by evolution. You are programmed to pursue the best mate you can get, a mate who increases the likelihood that your genes get passed down."

He tapped his tablet, signally he was done and said, "One last thing: as you are out there hooking up – I mean experimenting with your sexuality, remember, to use protection and that 'no' means 'no'."

Dr. Weber understood mate selection theory, but it did not fit his experience with Elizabeth. His experience was love at first sight. And it was not love of her waist-to-hip ratio – after all, she had been sitting behind a desk when they had met.

It was her eyes.

He thought about their first date and the hours they had spent talking. They had so much in common – a connection that was more than sexual. They were driven to accomplish their goals, they shared similar tastes; even on their first date, they had finished each other's sentences. They had agreed early in their relationship that they did not want children. When she had said she would move into his apartment, he had never been happier. His love for Elizabeth was sublime. Evolved packs of neurons could not explain the way he felt.

Chapter 14

That certainly wasn't what Mom taught me about sex, thought Natalie as she left the auditorium and stepped into the cool fall air.

She thought about what Dr. Weber had said about females preferring mates who were good providers. It made sense. When she and Rachel had fantasized about getting married, they had always imagined their husbands as rich and handsome providers, with nice homes and the best clothes. Natalia and Rachel had imagined themselves driving nice mini-vans filled with well-dressed and well-behaved children.

Gender roles?

She had learned that to be a high value mate for a good Christian man she needed to be a submissive, modest, and holy virgin who was good around the house. She was taught to pray for a husband who was kind, a hard worker who loved God, and was nice to his parents. Her mom told her once to look for a man who could admit it when he was wrong.

Clear skin, full lips, clear eyes, good teeth, large breasts, and the right waist-to-hip ratio?

She thought that when she got back to the dorm, she would measure her waist and hips and calculate the ratio.

Just curious.

She remembered once, when she was walking home from soccer practice, a construction worker had whistled at her and shouted, "Hey baby, you've got all the right curves in all the right places." Of course, she had ignored it, but secretly it had made her feel grown up.

As she entered the Quad, she could hear the Cowboy preaching from the Arch. The color of the leaves reminded Natalia of her grandmother's quilts, each leaf like a carefully selected fabric square. She looked around for Box. She wanted to talk to him about the things Dr. Weber had said and to talk to him about Gladys and all the red heads from the magazines on the Gladys' walls.

Box was there. He was with another man near Natalia's bench. He was speaking into a radio while the other man spread pine straw in a flowerbed.

"Okay," she heard Box say, "I'll send Sam to take care of it. Over and out."

The younger man was dressed like Box in green work pants and work shirt. His embroidered name badge read *Sam*. Box introduced him to Natalia.

"Natalia, this is Sam. Sam, this is my friend, Natalia Sanders. She's in my Sunday school class."

Sam brushed his hands on his pants, offered one to Natalia, and said, "How do you do, Miss Sanders?"

Natalia thought he looked like a younger version of Box. She guessed he was in his early thirties.

"Nice to meet you, Sam. Please, call me Natalia."

"Nice to meet you, Natalia," he repeated. "Henry is a good Sunday school teacher, isn't he?" he asked. "Were you in his class?"

"I was," he answered.

Box interrupted, "Sam, they need you over at the Student Union to show them where to spread the mulch."

"Yes sir." Sam said, "Nice to meet you, Natalia," as he climbed into the cart and drove away.

Box sighed and said, "It seems like I spend half my time on the radio and the other half doing paperwork." He motioned toward Natalia's bench. "Sam is a good man. He's a Christian. He met his wife in Sunday school. Now they have two young sons."

He sat with a bigger sigh and patted the bench for Natalia to sit beside him.

She asked, "Where are you when you aren't putting up little fences on the Quad? I haven't seen you around."

"Well," he leaned back and said, "You probably don't know it, and I'm not bragging, but I'm responsible for the whole landscape maintenance department at State U."

"I didn't know. That's impressive. So, you're really a big shot, huh?" she teased.

"I guess so," he chuckled. "I never wanted to be anybody's boss and I certainly never wanted a desk job, but when the president offered me the job, I knew I wasn't getting any younger and I wanted to give my children a chance to go to college. So I told him I would take the job, but only if I could keep taking care of the Quad myself."

"And he said yes?" she asked.

"He did. God worked it out and gave me good people like Sam to help me."

Box slowly looked from one end of the Quad to the other, as if seeing memories. "I probably spent as much time taking care of these plants and flowers and trees as I did my own children. When the children were young, Michelle would bring them here. They would run and play while Michelle read and I worked – such good times."

He looked at Natalia and said, "These days, God meets me here and we talk while I work. God is good."

The radio squawked with Sam's voice announcing his arrival at the student union. Box replied, "10-4," then looked at Natalia and said, "Sam is a good man. I hope he gets my job when I retire next year."

"You're retiring?" she whined.

"Yes. Michelle and I want to travel a bit and visit our grandchildren. I want to see Yellowstone again before I die. And when I get back, I'm going to ask Sam for a part time job so I can keep taking care of the Quad." He winked and smiled at Natalia. "Michelle doesn't know about that part of the plan. But enough about me – how are you adjusting to college life, Natty Rose?"

"Well," she said, "my roommate is creeping me out and my psychology professor is teaching me some whacked out stuff. But other than that, I love it."

"Gladys, right?"

He remembered her name.

"Yes. She's drinking and smoking marijuana, and the other night, she came into my room and was watching me sleep. And yesterday, the door to her room was open, and I could see she had hung pictures of red-haired women all over her walls. It's really creeping me out. I'm a red head and I live next door." She sighed. "I'm worried about her, Box, and I don't know what to do."

Box said, "That's hard. Let's pray."

"Here? For Gladys? Now?" she asked.

"Yes, for Gladys, but for you, too. And what better time than right now? That girl needs help, Natalia. Did it ever occur to you that of all the girls who might have been your suitemate, that maybe you got Gladys for a reason? We need to pray for her and we need to pray for God's wisdom and direction for you."

He did not give her time to answer. There on the Quad, oblivious to students walking by, Box slid from the bench down to his knees and started to pray. Natalia bowed her head. Box thanked God for Gladys and for Natalia, and he thanked God for what He was going to do for Gladys through Natalia. He prayed for healing for Gladys and for confidence and wisdom and protection for Natalia. Then he was finished. It took almost as long for him to get onto his knees and back up again as it did for him to pray.

They sat quietly for a while. It was a comfortable quiet. Then Natalia wondered aloud, "Student Services has counseling for students, right?"

"They do," he answered. "Kathy Hill is the director. You may have met her – she's in the choir at Calvary Way."

"I haven't met her, but I think I should see her to talk to her about Gladys," she said.

"Good idea," Box said. "And keep praying."

You mean start praying.

"I will," she said. Natalia felt guilty that she had not already been praying for Gladys. She realized that since she'd been at college, she hadn't been praying very much at all, except at mealtime. And even then it was quick and silent, so as not to attract attention.

Box changed the subject and asked, "So what is old Ernst – I mean, Dr. Weber, teaching these days?"

"Just sex and hooking up and evolution and how dumb Christians are." She shrugged.

"Same old Dr. Weber," he said. He poked her with his elbow to get her to smile.

"I've been interested in psychology since high school," said Natalia. "I was looking forward to taking it, it seemed so interesting. I thought I would learn why people do the things they do, like why is my little brother such a pest? I mean, I like the study groups and the textbook is interesting, but Dr.

Weber's lectures are such a bummer. He makes me feel so…" she searched for the right word. "Cheap! He makes me feel cheap. And he seems so angry."

Box looked as though he was reliving a painful memory. He shook his head and said, "Dr. Weber has been running from God for a long time, and that takes its toll." His smile came back and he said, "But there's always hope. God can change even the hardest heart. I'm proof that God changes hard hearts. Elizabeth, Mrs. Weber, is proof, too. Today she is a sweet, kind, and gentle soul, but before – well, you heard her testimony. She persecuted believers, and she almost got me fired for talking about Jesus."

"There's always hope," Natalia repeated.

"I met Ernst and Elizabeth when he was a new associate professor and Elizabeth was still in law school. When they got married, over there," he pointed toward the fountain in the center of the Quad, "I helped set up the tables and chairs. Michelle and the kids came."

Natalia looked at the fountain and imagined getting married there.

"Ernst took it hard when Elizabeth was saved, but the angels rejoiced," he said with a sigh and a smile. "The problem with Dr. Weber is he's not humble. He thinks he has it all figured out, but he doesn't. He believes he is the authority on why we're here, how we got here, and what happens when we die. But he needs God as his ultimate authority."

He checked his watch and asked, "When is your next class? I don't want to make you late."

"It's at eleven. I still have some time," she answered.

He continued, "Ernst used to tell me that faith is belief in spite of the lack of evidence. Does he still say that?"

"Yes," she said. "On the first day."

"I told him once, a long time ago, that I admired *his* great faith. I said, 'Ernst, you've got more faith than anybody I know.' That made him mad." Box laughed again and in a poor imitation of a German accent said, 'What are you talking about, Henry? You are the Christian, not me. I don't have faith – I have science.' But the way I see it, he has more faith than anybody. It takes big faith to believe that everything came from nothing – that the universe just appeared and the Earth just happened to be perfectly suited for life. It takes big faith to believe that proteins and DNA and cells and organs and plants and animals and you and I are products of undirected, natural processes. Dr. Weber, of all people, with all his knowledge about the complexity of the brain, should know that it didn't just happen. It's not that simple. It takes a lot of faith to see all the evidence of design and not believe there is a designer. I think in his heart, Dr. Weber knows that. He just can't admit it."

Natalia said, "You would be a good professor."

"Ha! I would get fired for talking about Jesus and leaving class to rake leaves." He turned his body toward Natalia and patted her on the shoulder. "But thanks for saying so. I thought about it. I had the G.I. bill and thought about going to graduate school and teaching horticulture. But I met Michelle and we got married and had our first son. That seemed more important."

"I bet you were a good dad. I want to meet your wife. Michelle, right?"

"Yes. She keeps the babies in the nursery during church, but Sunday I can take you down to meet her. You will like her," he said. "I tell her about the prayer requests from Sunday school and we pray for them together."

"How did you meet her?" she asked.

"Right here," he said.

"You met at State U.?"

"Yes, at State U., but right here," he said, pointing to the bench on which they were sitting. "She was sitting on this very bench. That's why I think of this bench as mine. I was walking down the Quad on my way to the library. I remember seeing her. She was reading a book. The way the sun was shining through the trees, it looked like God had shined a spotlight on her to say, 'Hey Henry, look here!'"

"Aww," said Natalia. "That's so romantic."

"With every step my eyes got wider and my throat got tighter. She was the most beautiful girl I had ever seen. Still is."

Natalia asked, "What did you say to her?"

"I didn't say anything. I was trying to look at her without her seeing me looking, and I tripped."

"You tripped? That was smooth."

"I didn't just trip. I fell down and my books scattered all over the place." He pointed to the sidewalk in front of them.

Natalia laughed. "Then what happened?"

"She looked up from her book and looked at me – into my eyes. She asked if I was all right and helped me pick up my books. One of the books I dropped was C.S. Lewis' *Mere Christianity*, and guess what?" he asked. "That's what she was reading." He laughed. "She was so pretty. She asked if I was a Christian. I said 'yes,' but it sounded more like a mouse's squeak than a 225-pound boxer. When she smiled at me and said, 'I am, too,' and showed me her book, it was all over. I've loved her ever since."

"Ah, that's so sweet," said Natalia as she stood. "You're a big shot romantic. I can't wait to meet her. I have to go to class now. Thanks for talking with me about Gladys and stuff. I'm going to go to the health center after class to talk with Ms. Hill."

Box slowly stood. It looked to Natalia like it was painful. He said, "I'm praying for you, Natalia."

"Thank you, Box. See you later."

During English class, Natalia thought about what she would say to Ms. Hill. After class, she walked back across the Quad, toward the Student Union building. During freshman orientation, her guide had called the Student Union the campus living room, a place where students could socialize, eat frozen yogurt, attend special events, and even go bowling. The Lewis Health and Wellness Center took up the entire third floor. It provided non-emergency medical care and mental health counseling, but its main service was providing birth control and abortion referrals.

Unlike the warm and inviting feel of the campus living room downstairs, the Health and Wellness Center looked more like a doctor's office or hospital. Natalia followed the signs to Counseling Services. The lobby was empty except for a receptionist sitting behind a counter. Her badge read *Stephanie*, and she looked to Natalia like she was a student, too. Stephanie was typing something on her phone and did not acknowledge Natalia.

Natalia cleared her throat.

"May I help you?" Stephanie said, without looking up.

"Hi. My name is Natalia Sanders. I'm here to speak to Kathy Hill, please – about my suitemate."

"Okay," she said as she glanced up at Natalia and handed her a clipboard, all while typing with her free thumb. "Have a seat over there and fill out these forms, front and back, sign where highlighted, and someone will be with you soon."

Do I look like I need counseling?

"Um," said Natalia as she took the clipboard. "I am not here for an appointment. I just need to talk to her about my suitemate."

Stephanie looked up long enough to roll her eyes and say, "Your *suitemate*. Of course. It does not matter whom you want to talk about. Everybody has to do the paperwork, ma'am, it's protocol." She flashed a fake smile and went back to her typing.

She called me ma'am.

"But," Natalia protested, "my friend Henry Brown –
he's head of the landscape maintenance department
at State U. – said Ms. Hill might know how I can help
my suitemate. Her name is Gladys."

Stephanie frowned at something on her phone.
"There's no need to get upset, ma'am. It is protocol.
I'll also need a copy of your driver's license, student
ID, and insurance card – if you have one."

"But, it's not about me," Natalia said. "It's my
suitemate." She thought that going to Student
Services was not a good idea after all.

"Listen," said Stephanie as she put down her phone
and for the first time really looked at Natalia. "I
believe that you are here to talk about your suitemate.
Whatever. But everybody fills out the paperwork. It
is protocol. And if it really is your suitemate, she is
going to have to come in herself. Confidentiality and
all. Be sure she brings a copy of her driver's license,
student ID, and insurance card, if she has one. Oh,
and we close at 4:30."

Natalia felt helpless. She said, "Okay. Never mind.
Thank you." She returned the clipboard and left.

It should be easier to get someone some help, she
thought as she made her way back to her dorm.

Natalia had not been back in her room long when
there was a knock on the bathroom door.

"Natty Rose, can I come in?" It was Gladys. "I need your help."

What a relief.

"Sure Gladys, I'll help you. Come in."

Natalia started to tell Gladys about Kathy Hill and the need to bring her license and ID and insurance card, when Gladys said, "I need you to help me catch whoever is pranking me."

"What?" Natalia asked, trying not to look confused.

"Somebody is pranking me. They stand outside my door and say 'Gladys, Gladys. We know you're in there, Gladys,' but when I open the door, no one is there. They run away. It's not funny and I need you to help me catch them."

Gladys looked frightened. Natalia was frightened too, but tried not to show it.

"Okay, Gladys, I'll listen for them. But I know this lady at counseling services, maybe she can help."

"No," Gladys said as she turned to leave. "I just need them to quit pranking me so I can get some sleep. I'll be fine."

Natalia stood staring into the bathroom and wondered what to do. It did not occur to her to pray.

Chapter 15

It could be worse, Nathan thought as he marked the 6:15pm study subject absent. It was the third no-show of the day.

"Does this happen often?" asked Natalia. "Last week, everyone showed up."

"It happens too often," he said. "When the mothers sign up for the study, we ask them to call to let us know if their child gets sick or something else comes up – but they usually don't. Sometimes the advancement of science grinds to a halt over a case of colic. It can be frustrating."

But Nathan was not frustrated that afternoon. The day was a bust for his research, but things were looking up for his love life. Three no-shows meant there was time to talk with Natalia – and he enjoyed that. He almost hoped the next baby would not show as well.

Natalia was different from most girls he had met at State University. She didn't talk about vampire love stories and she had never read the *Harry Potter* books. She didn't constantly check her phone, and the whole time they talked, she did not send a single text message or stop to take a selfie. She didn't gossip about the girls back home. She did not ask if he thought she was pretty or if he liked her outfit. She did not talk about her new diet or old boyfriend, and she didn't say 'like' in every sentence. She didn't lecture him about feminism or politics, and even though she was a Christian, she did not preach.

She was a good listener, too. He told her the real reason he was a troublemaker in school, and how he had felt when his parents sent him to military school. He even told her that he suspected his father had pulled strings to get him admitted to State University. She told him how she had felt closed-in by her small-town life back home, and of her dream to some day visit Paris. He told her about his trips there. She told him that her parents had wanted her to go to Bible college and to be a pastor's wife. He told her his parents wanted him to get an MBA and take over his father's factory. He told her that he had once wanted to get a fine arts degree in classical guitar, but decided to study psychology instead.

He wanted to tell her that he thought she was sexy.

Take it slow, he reminded himself.

Natalia said, "I wanted to learn to play the guitar, but my mom made me take piano lessons instead." She looked at the guitar in the corner. "Will you play a song?"

He hoped it wasn't too soon. He knew that most girls loved it when he played. He thought of his guitar as a babe magnet that turned young co-eds into putty in his hands. He knew it was working when their smiles turned dreamy, when they looked into his eyes, sighed, and tilted their heads. He thought that someday, when he was a professor and could choose what research he did, he would explore the evolution of girls' attraction to guitar players.

"Sure, I'll play something," he said.

He got his guitar and started strumming softly. It was background music, soft enough so they could keep talking.

Natalia smiled, sighed, and tilted her head. "I just love the guitar."

Works every time, he thought.

"So, you're a Christian?" He was not interested in talking about religion. He got enough of that from Box. But he needed to gauge how much of a barrier religion would be to hooking up.

"I am," she answered. She looked puzzled. "Why do you ask?"

"It's just that I don't know many Christians. I mean, I've heard the Cowboy shouting and waving his Bible around."

"Did you think that all Christians wore cowboy hats and shouted Bible verses all day?" she asked.

"No, not all Christians. Have you met Henry Brown, the gardener? The one they call Box?" he asked.

"I know Box," she said. "He's my Sunday school teacher."

"I didn't know he was a Sunday school teacher, but I'm not surprised. Box always talks about Jesus, Jesus, Jesus, but he doesn't shout. He says, 'you need Jesus, Nate' and 'I'm praying for you, Nate.' But you're not like that."

She looked away and seemed upset.

"No, offense," he said quickly.

"I'm not offended," she said. "I think Box is great. I just wish I was more like him. As Christians, we are supposed to talk about Jesus and tell people about Him. I don't agree with the Cowboy's approach, but I admire his boldness." She paused. "What about you? What do you believe?"

"Well," he said, as he stopped strumming the guitar. "My parents were atheists, so I grew up an atheist, but I like to think of myself as agnostic – leaning toward atheism. I don't know whether God exists or not, but when I look around, I don't see a lot of reasons to believe. I mean, the Golden Rule and love your neighbor is good stuff, but there has been a lot of pain and death in the name of God. I'm like

Gandhi. Maybe I could be a Christian if it weren't for all the Christians."

He smiled and started to strum again. "And when we die, I don't know. I guess we are just gone. Don't get me wrong, I'm not like Dr. Weber. I do not hate religion or think that all religious people are dumb. I think that religion has benefits. I mean, except for things like the Crusades, the Inquisition, and the Salem Witch Trials, religion has done a lot of good. It provides comfort and hope that there is something after this life."

Natalia said, "I don't know many 'agnostics leaning toward atheism'. Do they all play the guitar?"

"Just the cool ones," he said, as their smiles met.

"Do you sing, too?" she asked.

"Sometimes. When I was an undergrad, I played in bars to make money."

She made the red puppet say in a squeaky voice, "Sing us a song."

It's too soon.

"Okay," he said. "If you insist."

The puppet replied, "We insist!"

"Cute."

Nathan Sutton's secret weapon for attracting girls was playing his guitar *and* singing. It never failed. He looked into their eyes and watched for the signs of attraction – dilated pupils, flushed cheeks, twirling hair. Then he would lean in for the kiss.

He cleared his throat, looked into Natalia's eyes, and sang:

Crossroads, seem to come and go, yeah.
The gypsy flies from coast to coast
Knowing many, loving none,
Bearing sorrow havin' fun,
But back home he'll always run
To sweet Natalia... mmm...

Natalia's eyes opened wide. "Oh my gosh! Did you just make that up? What is that song?"

"It's called *Melissa*, by an old band called the *Allman Brothers*. I just changed the name – it still rhymed."

She looked uncomfortable. Maybe confused.

Slow down.

"I'm sorry if that was creepy putting your name in."

"No," she said, "it was nice. You have a beautiful voice."

"Thank you."

"It makes me wonder." She leaned back and crossed her arms across her chest.

"Wonder what?" he asked as he put the guitar back in the corner.

"It makes me wonder how you can play and sing so pretty, and still be an agnostic or atheist or whatever."

Nathan wondered if he had been out-maneuvered.

"What are you talking about?"

"The way you play and sing, Nathan. It's a real gift."

"What do you mean – a gift? I practiced. I learned."

She laughed, making *him* feel uncomfortable and confused for a change.

"I've been paying attention," she said. "I've been thinking about what Dr. Weber said and how he explains things. He would say that what you just did on that guitar evolved from some monkey-man banging on a log with a stick." She laughed more.

She's laughing at me.

"Are you laughing at me?" he asked. He suddenly felt less like the predator and more like Natalia's prey.

"Yes, I'm sorry. And that song – whatever the real words are – Dr. Weber would say that it is no different than some croaking bullfrog trying to find a mate. *Ribit, ribit.*"

She laughed even more.

Nathan felt his cheeks flush.

When was the last time someone made me blush?

"I don't understand how anyone believes that," she said. "Next to the word of God, music deserves the highest praise. The gift of language combined with the gift of song was given to man that he should proclaim the word of God through music. Martin Luther said that."

She is smart.

"I've never thought about it like that," he lied as he looked away. Honestly, it was something that he tried not to think about. It was one thing to make up plausible stories to explain why girls evolved to like guys in bands, but it begged bigger questions. How did music evolve in the first place?

Bach? Beethoven? Elvis? Sutton?

He tried not to think about how the evolution of music ignored an even bigger question. How did *language* evolve? How did numerous and successive slight modifications in the brain produce the complexity and adaptability of human language? And the evolution of language ignored the biggest question of all – consciousness.

How does music touch me if there is no me – if I am just a pack of neurons? Am I really just a pack of neurons?

He tried not to wonder how evolution produced Nathan Sutton's subjective experience of Nathan Sutton. Why did he think of himself as a person with a mind? Big questions like that were the reason he called himself an agnostic and not an atheist. His father had said that agnostics were atheists without guts.

He noticed the clock on the wall. The last baby did not come. Four no-shows in a row. He regained his composure and pretended to look offended. "So I sing like a croaking bullfrog?"

"No," she said and put her hand on his. "You sing like an angel. You know what I mean."

"I do."

I do.

"Since the last baby is a no-show, want to go get something to eat and talk some more? You haven't had the full State U. experience until you've had the chili cheese fries at *Papa Joe's*."

He was pleasantly surprised when she said, "Sure. Why not? But no chili cheese fries, please."

"Great," he said. "It's a date. I'll hook up – I mean, lock up."

Chapter 16

Sure, why not? A croaking bullfrog looking for a mate. "It's a date?" What were you thinking, young lady?

Natalia watched as Nathan locked up the baby lab.

He's cute when he blushes.

She felt bad for Nathan that no babies had shown up, but she had had fun and she was still getting paid.

We talked for four hours!

Besides Rachel, she could not remember a time she had talked with anyone for four hours. Nathan was different from the guys back home. He did not talk about cars, football, or video games, and he didn't say 'you know' in every sentence. His breath didn't smell funny, and he was a really good listener. She felt comfortable telling him how she felt about small town life and her dreams for the future. She thought about how he made playing the guitar seem effortless. She was trying to remember the words to the song he had sung when he said, "Okay, let's go."

Natalia's dad had always said that when she started dating, the boy should walk to the house and knock on the door. "Never go out with a guy who sits in the car and honks the horn," he had warned.

If Dad could see me now.

"Fall is my favorite season," she said, as they walked the length of the Quad, heading towards town. The air was cool, but comfortable. The red and yellow and orange of the changing leaves in the twilight gave the scene a magical look. The faux gas street lamps made her think of Narnia.

He said, "My favorite is spring, but fall is a close second, especially when it's like this. It looks unreal – almost magical."

Can he read my mind?

She hoped not, because as they walked, Natalia had many things on her mind at once.

No chaperone. What's my curfew? I didn't bring money. Will he walk me to the dorm? What if he tries something? What if he doesn't? What a great smile. What if Mom calls? He has blue eyes. I love blue eyes. I have to tell Rachel. Why did I wear these shoes?

She planned to find out the real words to the song – *Melissa* – and put it on her playlist. No one had ever played and sung for her before, and unless Nathan turned out to be a real jerk, she thought it would be a first that she remembered for a long time.

"Sweet Natalia."

She thought about what her mom would say if she could see her now. When she was little, Natalia had imagined that on her first date she would ride in a limousine and wear a long chiffon dress, her future husband would wear a tuxedo, and they would laugh and talk about their future.

I hope I don't say anything dumb.

When they arrived at the Arch, Nathan walked through and Natalia walked around.

Just co-workers going out after work.

The bright lights and cars and noise of town broke the enchantment. Nathan and Natalia crossed with the traffic light and walked the half block to *Papa Joe's*. Nathan held open the door and swept his free hand across this body in an exaggerated arc, inviting her in.

"Thank you, kind gentleman," she said in her best southern accent.

"You are most welcome, ma'am," he replied with a similarly bad imitation.

It was louder inside *Papa Joe's* than outside. The hostess said, "Hi, Nathan, it's good to see you again."

To Natalia, she said, "My name is Abigail, I don't think we've met."

Nathan said, "This is my friend, Natalia Sanders. She is helping with my research."

"Hi," said Natalia.

"Hi," said Abigail. "They're all back there waiting for you."

"Um, could we get a booth tonight?" Nathan asked. "It's just the two of us."

Just the two of us. Pairing up.

"Sure," Abigail said as she led them to a booth against the wall. As they passed the bar, Nathan waved to the bartender.

"Hi, Daniel," he said as they passed. The bartender looked at Natalia, smiled, and gave Nathan a thumb's up.

After they were seated, Natalia asked, "What did she mean, 'they're all waiting for you'?"

"The other TA's. We get together on Thursdays."

"That's right," she said. "You told me that." Natalia recognized the other teaching assistants at a long table in the back room waving for Nathan to join them. "Should we go sit with your friends?"

"No, but if you'll excuse me a minute, I want to tell them that I have other plans, tonight."

While she waited, Natalia looked around. The brick walls looked old and were covered with neon lights, road signs, parts from old cars, and lots and lots of old photographs. The photo on the wall of the booth was of an old man with a beautiful woman on each arm. It was signed, '*To Papa Joe.*' The crowd was young and everyone looked to be having a good time. Natalia hoped she did not look like a homeschooler. The waitresses wore short shorts, lots of makeup, and tight white tank tops tied in a knot on the bottom to show their belly button rings. She didn't recognize the music that was playing and thought it was too loud.

Restaurant? This is a bar.

Natalia had never been to a bar or even a restaurant that served alcohol. Her parents did not believe in patronizing businesses that sold alcohol. When their favorite grocery store started selling beer, her mom started shopping somewhere else. Even if they did not serve alcohol, Natalia's family would not have patronized *Papa's Joes,* because the waitresses dressed immodestly.

When Nathan came back, he put his hand on Natalia's shoulder, squeezed just a little, and said, "One more thing. I'll be right back." He took money from his wallet and fed it into the jukebox near the bar and pushed some buttons.

He was smiling as he came back and slid into the booth across from Natalia. He said, "Maybe if we're lucky it will play before we leave."

"What did you play?"

"*Melissa*, of course. I want you to hear the original."

The waitress came over and poured them each a glass of water. Then she asked, "A pitcher of the usual, Nathan?"

He answered, "No, Tiffany, just water for now, and a plate of the bacon wrapped dates. We'll order drinks, then."

Dates on our date.

Natalia watched as Tiffany walked away.

I would look good in those shorts.

"Hoochie coochie girl," Natalia said.

"What did you say?" asked Nathan with a puzzled frown.

"Hoochie coochie girl," she repeated. "It's what my dad always calls girls who dress immodestly." She made quotation marks in the air when she said, 'immodestly.'

"I guess hoochie coochie girls were old timey dancers or something," – Natalia continued. "It doesn't matter. It was always clear that being a hoochie coochie girl was not good."

Nathan said, "I like that word. Hoochie coochie, hoochie coochie." He watched as a waitress walked by. "Amy, she's one of the TAs, she hates coming here because of the way the waitresses dress. She says it objectifies and devalues women. I guess she's right. See my friend, Daniel, the bartender over there?" Nathan motioned toward the young man filling a pitcher with beer. "He told me that once the waitress got together – this was when Papa Joe was still alive – and told him that they didn't want to wear their shorts so short or their shirts so tight. So, Papa Joe let them. And you know what happened?"

"They made fewer tips?" she guessed.

"Yes. And they sold less beer and pizza. They voted to go back to 'hoochie coochie'."

"It proves that it is not about the food," she said.

He laughed. "It is ironic that at State U., with its enlightened knowledge and respect for women and feminism, the most popular bar in town is the one where the waitresses dress like hoochie coochie girls."

Tiffany returned with the dates.

Nathan said, "I'm going to have a beer. Would you like one?"

Did I think he wouldn't ask?

In that second, Natalia thought about everything she had been told about alcohol. It was time for her to decide for herself.

No.

She leaned forward and whispered so Tiffany could not hear, "I'm only 18."

He leaned in so they were eye to eye and said, "It's all right, I know the bartender. Besides, you look at least twenty-one or twenty-two."

Natalia sat back, shrugged, said, "Okay. Sure. Why not? I'll have whatever you're having."

"Tiffany, we'd like the strawberry ale, Red-Headed Woman." He winked at Natalia.

Don't blush.

"Two Read-Headed Women coming up," she said. Natalia and Nathan watched as Tiffany walked away.

"You want to hear a story?" Natalia asked.

"Yes. Tell me a story," he answered.

"When I was fifteen, my parents put me in the Christian school so I could play high school soccer. It had a strict dress code – stricter than my mom's. Shirts had to be long enough to cover your belly, even when you held your arms up." She raised her arms to demonstrate. "And skirts had to completely cover your knees. Well, one day, I wore my favorite denim skirt to school, and I guess I had gotten a little taller so it only covered half of my knee. The homeroom teacher sent me to the principal's office for a modesty check."

"Seriously? A modesty check?"

"Seriously. I had to get down on my knees. If the skirt had touched the floor, I would have been fine – but it didn't. So I had to go to the bathroom and put on a pair of ugly grey sweat pants under my skirt until my dad could bring jeans."

Tiffany returned with their beers.

"Thank you." They said in unison.

Beer smells like pee. Strawberry pee.

Nathan asked, "What did your dad say?"

"My dad is usually pretty laid back, but he got so mad, he was shaking. He told the principal that his daughter was no hoochie coochie girl and that she would not be back to that school. That was the end of my high school soccer career."

"That's crazy." Nathan sniffed his beer, and then took a drink.

"I guess," she said. "There has to be a balance. And it's not just clothes. My mom was strict about makeup, too. The only amount of makeup I was allowed to wear was just enough so it didn't look like I was wearing any. So, I just quit wearing it."

Nathan said, "Well, if it's any consolation, I don't think you need any makeup."

She was afraid she might blush. She felt pretty and she wanted to give him a kiss on the cheek for the nice compliment. She wondered what it would be like to really kiss him.

How Christian is that?

Natalia said, "I believe there are moral laws that apply to everyone. There are laws written on our hearts – our conscience. Your puppet study is proving that. But there are also a lot of man's rules about make-up and skirt length."

It seemed to Natalia that something she had said made Nathan uncomfortable. She thought that maybe she had violated a beer-drinking custom, so she held her breath and tasted beer for the first time.

"How do you like it?" he asked.

Yuck! She wanted to spit it out.

"It's interesting," she said.

I hate beer.

"I don't think I like strawberry in my beer. You can have it." She took a drink of water, ate a date, and changed the subject from beer. "So, what made you choose psychology over classical guitar?"

"That's a very good question. Part of the reason is that the only thing my parents hated worse than the idea of a degree in classical guitar was a degree in psychology." He took a big drink of beer. It looked to Natalia like he was thinking deeply about his answer. "I already told you that my parents and I weren't exactly close," he continued. "When I was young, ten or eleven, I remember thinking that if I could just be good enough – if I could just say or do the right thing – maybe they wouldn't yell so much."

Natalia imaged Nathan at ten years old trying to be good enough. It was cute, but sad. She said, "Aww. That's so sad."

"I know, right? Sad. But that's not the main reason. I finally figured out that it wasn't my problem that my parents didn't like each other and had no business having a kid. But the main reason I chose psychology was a man I saw sometimes when I went to town with my nanny."

"You had a nanny?"

"Yes, I had a nanny. Born with a silver spoon in my mouth, as they say. Don't interrupt."

"Sorry. Go on."

"There was a man in town. His name was Hobert Grasty. The kids teased him and called him 'Nasty Grasty.' Whenever I saw him, he looked like he was having a conversation with someone. He would sit on a bench and talk and talk –- to no one I could see. When he was looking for cans in the trash, he was talking the whole time. I tried to listen. It sounded like gibberish. But I could tell by his inflection and tone that he was asking and answering questions, and sometimes he argued and cried and shouted. It was as if I was hearing one side of a two-way conversation. I never knew what Hobart was saying, but I could tell it was important – to him."

Sensitive.

"Think about it. What's more interesting than studying people? Psychology is cool. It fascinates me. The human mind is amazing."

Your eyes are amazing.

"You may not know it, but long before psychology was modernized, theologians and philosophers were already writing about the mind – about what it means to be human."

Smart.

Nathan set off on an explanation of how psychology "lost its soul" when it adopted strict naturalistic presuppositions. Natalia did not understand some of what he said, but she could tell it was important to him. She enjoyed watching him talk. She felt warm and she could not stop smiling.

She jumped when he said, "That's it!" and pointed toward the jukebox. "*The Allman Brothers. Melissa.*"

He stopped talking and finished Natalia's beer as they listened to the music over the noise of *Papa Joe's.*

She liked Nathan's version of the song better. When it was over, she said, "That was good. That guy didn't sound at all like a bull frog."

"I guess that's why Gregg Allman is famous and I'm not. Do you want to get something to eat besides these dates?

No. I want to walk around town and hold your hand and listen to you talk and for you to sing another song.

"No, I have some studying to do. I'm feeling a little sleepy and I have to get up early. I should go back to the dorm now."

"Okay. Can I walk you back?"

You better.

"You don't have to."

"I want to."

"Okay."

They did not walk through the Quad on the way to Laurel dorm. They took the long way around campus, and as they walked, they looked in the shop windows and laughed about vampire romance novels and hoochie coochie clothes. Her fingers felt tingly and it wasn't even cold outside. She felt pretty and she noticed other couples.

We're *a couple.*

Some couples walked arm in arm and some held hands. She wanted to hold Nathan's hand.

"Be ye not unequally yoked together with unbelievers: for what fellowship hath righteousness with unrighteousness and what communion hath light with darkness?"

Sometimes she wished she did not know so many Bible verses.

"I need your advice about my suitemate," she said, bringing her thoughts back from Nathan's hand on her shoulder at the bar. "She has mental problems. I went to Health Services, but they were not helpful." She tried to pay attention while he explained the nature of thought disorders and the problem of treatment compliance, but their hands kept touching as they walked.

"Come on. I want to show you something," he said as he grabbed her hand and pulled her toward New Campus. He slowed their pace as they approached the Psychology – Literature complex, but he did not let go of her hand until he needed his key to unlock a side door.

"Are we breaking and entering?" she asked, thinking how exciting it would be if he said yes.

So exciting!

"It's not breaking and entering if you have a key," he said as he unlocked the door. He took her by the hand and led her down a short hallway and though another door into a large open room. There was little light, but she recognized they were on the stage in the psychology auditorium.

"Cover your eyes," he warned as he flipped on the lights.

As her eyes adjusted, she could see her seat in the middle row of the middle section. Nathan stood behind the lectern. It looked as though he was imagining a room full of students.

"I get a real adrenaline rush when I'm up here," he said, without looking at her. "It's the same as when I'm about to play guitar for an audience. It's fun. Come try it."

Natalia took his place at Dr. Weber's lectern. She imagined a class of one hundred fifty students looking at her.

I would throw up.

"I would be too nervous."

"Maybe, but you seem pretty bold."

Bold?

"Ha! I would throw up."

Natalia giggled and tried to speak with a German accent. "Faith is belief despite the lack of evidence." She pointed at Nathan and said loudly, "You are nothing, nothing but a pack of neurons."

They laughed together and mocked Dr. Weber as they left the auditorium. They talked less as they walked the rest of the way to Natalia's dorm. Nathan took her hand a third time and they swung arms as they walked. When they arrived, Natalia felt bolder.

Bold!

"You should come with me."

"Come where?" he asked.

"To Sunday school – Box's class. It's really good."

"Sounds interesting. Maybe I will...sometime."

We could sit together.

"You could go to church with me, too. The music in the early service is great. You'd like it."

We could hold hands there, too.

"Maybe I will," he said.

"You can wear your blue blazer," she laughed as she bumped him off the walkway with her shoulder.

"Hey!" he said, with his hands on his hips. "Are you making fun of my blazer?"

Athletic body.

She extended her right hand and said, "Maybe a little. This is where I live. I had a good time. Thank you."

He smiled and took her hand in both of his. He shook her hand and said, "Thank you. I had fun, too. See you next week. Maybe I'll take you up on your offer. Though, I've never gone on a date to church." He smiled again and backed away." He said, "good night," waved, turned, and walked away.

Natalia ran up the stairs and down the hall to her room. When she was inside, she leaned against the door, exhaled, and squealed.

She tried to call Rachel. She wanted to tell her she was dating, too, but the call went to voicemail. Natalia paced and twirled around her room, downloaded her new favorite song, and played it over and over again. As she got ready for bed, she analyzed the hidden meaning of every word Nathan had said that night.

When she finally fell asleep, she dreamed she was a waitress at *Papa Joe's*, and she was making really good tips. In her dream, one of the teaching assistants pinched her butt and she dropped a tray of beers. Everyone laughed.

She woke to real crashing noises and real laughter and light from under the bathroom door. She lay quietly and listened. It was Gladys – giggling and whispering loudly and banging into things. And there was something else.

There is a guy in there.

Natalia pulled the covers over her head and tried not to listen.

Chapter 17

The next Sunday morning, Natalia called her mom as she walked to church. She was feeling drowsy. She had not slept well the past two nights -- since *Papa Joe's*. She had thought about skipping church.

"Good morning, Mom."

"Good morning, Natty Rose."

Always cheerful.

"I've missed talking to you. I was worried. How are you doing? Are you on your way to Church?"

I should just blurt it out.

"I'm fine, Mom."

Mom, I went on a date.

"I'm walking to church now."

With a boy.

"Yes, I'm meeting nice people."

To a bar.

"Yes, I'm looking forward to fall break."

And I drank beer.

"My job is good, Mom."

He's good looking.

"My classes are fine, Mom."

But he's not a Christian.

"I'm fine, Mom. Really."

We held hands.

"Thanks for praying, Mom."

I would have let him kiss me if he tried.

"I love you, too, Mom."

I miss you, Mom.

"Bye, Mom."

Natalia felt uncomfortable during the church service. She didn't clap and sway along with the choir. She felt like Box was looking at her. The sermon that morning was about sex. God's plan for sex. Marriage – an expression of God-like intimacy and unity, not to be mistaken for lust.

Come on, God, it was just a date.

She had heard many sermons about sex and marriage, but she had never really listened before.

Sure, he's good looking, but I'm not in lust.

It took extra effort to resist the tug she felt during the altar call.

Just co-workers hanging out after work.

She thought about going back to the dorm and skipping Sunday school, but she knew Box had seen her and she did not want to have to explain her absence later. She regretted her decision to stay when, after prayer time, Box led the class in more discussion about sex and lust and being unequally yoked.

"What are the challenges to staying pure in the culture at State University?" Box asked.

A guy said, "It's difficult. Sex is in our face all the time, on TV, in movies and magazines, and the Internet."

A girl said, "It's like you're a freak if you're a virgin at our age."

"Waiting is hard."

"Everybody is doing it."

Natalia chewed her fingernails.

Box said, "I understand. It is hard to stay pure. However, you do not have to conform to the ways of this world. The Bible is clear. Sex is intended for marriage. You are bombarded by a culture that says sex is okay, as long as you love each other. Well, it's not. It is God's will that you should be sanctified – to not just avoid sexual immorality, but to flee from it. Control your body in a way that is holy and honorable, not like this lustful culture. There will be temptation and desire – you would be a fool to think there won't be. Purity is hard work."

I've got this.

"Ask someone to hold you accountable."

Rachel is dating, too.

"Run from temptation, not toward it. Run to win the race of sexual purity."

I've got this. Really.

She thought about her purity ring.

What else would I have let him do?

It was not often that God spoke directly to Natalia. But there, in the basement of Calvary Way, she heard Him, as clear to her heart as Box's voice to her ears.

He reminded her of Jeremiah 29:11-13. She had memorized those verses a long time ago.

"For I know the thoughts that I think toward you, saith the Lord, thoughts of peace, and not of evil, to give you an expected end. Then shall ye call upon me, and ye shall go and pray unto me, and I will hearken unto you. And ye shall seek me, and find me, when ye shall search for me with all your heart."

Fine.

She folded her arms across her chest with a huff.

I won't go out with him again. He probably won't ask, anyway.

She saw Box watching her.

When she got back to the dorm, Gladys was there. Her door was open and Natalia saw her sitting on the edge of her bed.

"Hi, Gladys. Where have you been? Are you okay?"

Gladys looked in Natalia's direction and said, "Oh, hi. I met a guy. We've been partying. He's a tattoo artist. I got a new tattoo on my shoulder. See?"

She slid one strap of her tank top off her shoulder.

Rob?

"What does it say?"

"Rob. That's his name."

"You met a guy and you let him tattoo his name on your shoulder?"

I can't wait to tell Rachel.

"It was free," she shrugged. "I'm going to sleep now."

Natalia was careful to lock her side of the bathroom door as she left.

Chapter 18

At 9:15am, Dr. Weber drank the last sip of his coffee and kicked open the metal door to the E. G. Boring Psychology Auditorium.

Brandy makes coffee better.

"Today our topic is mental illness," he said in greeting to his students, "more accurately called *psychopathology.* In the Christian Bible, the book of Mark, the fifth chapter, Jesus is said to have healed a man possessed by demons." He paused to open his notes. "It's a funny story, you all should read it. It is a good illustration of one of countless primitive explanations of mental illness. Throughout history, mankind has struggled to understand mental illness – to understand what goes wrong with the brain and what to do about it. But fortunately today, no one with any intelligence believes that demons and gods or the moon and stars have anything to do with mental illness."

So, what went wrong with Elizabeth?

He asked himself that question a lot lately.

"Today, we understand that mental illnesses are complex neurobiological phenomena with strong genetic and environmental influences. Mental illness, just like mental health, exists in the brain."

Maybe it's hormones. Maybe she will snap out of it.

But he knew that his wife's faith in Jesus was not something she was likely to 'snap out' of. It had been three years.

"Clinical and counseling psychologists have made great progress in the diagnosis, care, and treatment of mental illness. But our interest is in the seemingly special challenge mental illness presents to our evolutionary paradigm."

Dr. Weber noticed Nathan at the far end of the front row typing on his phone. He made a mental note to yell at him later.

"Consider schizophrenia. Schizophrenia is a terribly debilitating illness. It causes psychosis; sufferers experience hallucinations. They hear things – voices. They experience delusions. Their thinking is bizarre and disorganized, and their behavior is often disruptive and disturbing, making it difficult to live and function. For these reasons, through history, people with schizophrenia have had shorter life expectancies. Today, someone with schizophrenia dies on average twenty-five years earlier than people without schizophrenia. Second, they reproduce at lower rates. The nature of the disease makes it less likely that someone with schizophrenia will find a mate and produce offspring. In evolutionary terms, they are not exactly high value mates."

200

Why do I care what she believes?

"Therein lies the dilemma. Why hasn't evolution selected against the genes for schizophrenia?"

I should just move out.

"We would predict that evolution would select against the genes for schizophrenia, but it hasn't. Why not? There are several plausible explanations. Perhaps what we call the symptoms of mental illness were once beneficial traits that persist in the genome today. Perhaps having a family member with schizophrenia provided an evolutionary advantage for the group – it facilitated the reproductive success of the kin. Perhaps it is epigenetic – a heritable byproduct, if you will, of some other beneficial adaptation. I prefer the theory that schizophrenia is a new mutation and there just hasn't been enough time for evolution to eliminate it."

Like religion.

Dr. Weber's attention, along with that of everyone else, was drawn to the back row of the auditorium to the girl with straight black hair and tattoos. She was crying and mumbling as she scrambled over the back of her chair and ran head long into the exit door.

Dr. Weber felt irritated by the interruption.

With the click of the door closing behind her, every head in the auditorium turned back toward Dr. Weber.

He asked, "Does anyone know that young lady?"

The red head in the middle seat stood and said, "I do. She's my suitemate. I should check on her."

"Thank you, you are dismissed" Dr. Weber said.

Natalia quickly gathered her things and climbed the stairs to leave.

Chapter 19

Natalia stepped out of the auditorium and shielded her eyes from the sun and looked for Gladys.

Where would she go?

She slung her backpack over her shoulder and walked quickly toward the dorm. Gladys' door was open. "Gladys. Gladys," she called, but Gladys was not there.

Maybe she went to health services.

As she hurried back across campus, Natalia finally found Gladys sitting on Natalia's favorite bench near the psychology department. Box was with there, too.

Natalia slowed her approach and watched. Gladys was rocking back and forth, her head was down, and her hands covered her face. Box had one hand on her shoulder and the other hand lifted a little, palm up. Natalia knew he was praying.

Gladys was crying. Box looked tired. Through her tears, she was saying, "I'm a byproduct. They know it's me!"

Natalia remembered what Gladys had said. *"When I'm high I don't hear them."* She understood.

Gladys has schizophrenia.

She felt pity for Gladys.

What else could I have done for her?

Box looked toward Natalia and motioned with his upturned hand for her to come. Natalia sat beside Gladys on the bench. "Gladys, it's me, Natty Rose. It's okay, Gladys. It's going to be all right."

Gladys stopped crying and looked up. She stared at Natalia and then Box. "I'm okay," she said, wiping the tears with her arm, smearing mascara across her cheeks. "I thought Weber was talking about me. The voices told me he was talking about me, but I'm all right now – they stopped."

She took Box's hand and said, "Thank you for praying for me, sir. I think it helped."

She looked at Natalia and forced a smile. "I'm sorry, Natty Rose. Its been getting bad again, but it's not the first time. I should have told you. I'm supposed to be on medications for my thinking, but I stopped taking them. I didn't want to be that kid on psych meds." She sighed. "It was going good at first. Then getting drunk and stoned helped for a while. But now the voices are telling me to cut myself again – or worse."

Natalia saw Dr. Weber and Nathan walking toward them. It looked to her like Dr. Weber was scolding

Nathan. Dr. Weber passed them by without looking their way. Nathan stopped and stood beside Box.

Natalia put her hand on Gladys' shoulder and said, "It's okay Gladys. You'll be all right. Can I walk with you to the Health Center to get help?"

Gladys nodded.

Box said, "I'll call on the radio and let them know you're coming."

Nathan said, "I'll go with you."

It was a short walk to the Student Center. Gladys was chatty – focused on what was about to happen. She told Nathan and Natalia that there would be security guards when they got to the clinic and that she had to stay calm so they didn't restrain her. She said, "It's also important not to back talk to the deputy that drives you to the hospital or they might make you wear handcuffs the whole way."

I'll remember that.

"This will be my seventh hospitalization. It will take a long time to find a hospital that takes my insurance. The good thing is that they'll give me a shot of something and I'll get a good nap. I'll be all right," she reassured Natalia. "Would you go to my room and get the bag with my clothes and bring it to me?"

"I will." Natalia promised.

"I thought Weber was talking about me," Gladys continued. "I have schizophrenia," she said with a deep sigh.

"It will be okay," Natalia said. She thought it sounded trite.

As they approached the Student Union, they made their way through a group of students gathered outside. They rode the elevator to the third floor where they were met by a lady with a clipboard and two nervous looking campus security guards. Stephanie, the receptionist from Natalia's first visit, was not there.

"Hi, Gladys," said the lady. "My name is Kathy Hill. My friend, Henry Brown called to say you were coming. Can we go to my office and talk?"

She's the redhead from the choir!

As she followed Kathy Hill to her office, Gladys looked at her and said, "I love your hair. I love red hair."

Natalia tried to smile as she waved and said, "Bye, Gladys. Get well soon."

Get well soon? What a dumb thing to say.

She felt like crying for Gladys' sake.

Bless her heart.

She thought about asking Nathan for a hug.

Can I have a hug? And by the way, I can't date you because you're not a Christian.

Natalia and Nathan took the stairs back down. They did not talk. As they stepped from the stairwell, she saw that the crowd had grown large, organized, and loud.

"Pride parade," Nathan shouted to Natalia.

"What's that?" she shouted back.

"Gay pride rally and parade. They're celebrating legalized gay marriage. Let's go over there and watch for a minute."

Another first.

"Just for a minute," she said, "I promised to get Gladys' clothes."

She followed him up a small hill to a shady spot with a view. Nathan he sat down on the grass. Natalia sat beside him, but not too close.

Below them, the plaza and sidewalk had filled with people – Natalia guessed five hundred at least – carrying signs and rainbow banners and laughing and hugging. A lady with a microphone was making a speech.

The Cowboy was there, too. Natalia pointed him out to Nathan. People were actually listening to him preach. He shouted and they shouted back, which energized him to shout louder still. Natalia guessed they took exception to the Cowboy's message of eternal damnation for homosexuals. The whole scene made her laugh.

"Why are you laughing?" Nathan asked. He looked confused.

"I don't know. It seems silly, I guess – all the shouting."

He smiled and their eyes met. All thought of telling him that she could not date him disappeared.

"What do you think?" she asked. "About gay marriage, I mean."

"Well, it's complicated," he said. "On the one hand, I don't understand same sex attraction, but who am I to judge?" He stretched out on his back with his head resting in his hands.

Don't stare.

"Dr. Weber told me once that homosexuality had to be a choice," Nathan continued, "that it couldn't be inborn or genetic. He said that any genetic trait that decreases the chance of reproductive success, be it schizophrenia or homosexuality, would be selected against by evolution."

Natalia struggled to pay attention to his words.

"There are other theories, though. Some people suggest that homosexuals increase the reproductive and survival rates of other members of the gene pool. I don't know. Live and let live, I always say. What about you? What do you think?"

He rolled onto his side to face her, which made it hard for her to think of something to say.

She said, "I'm not sure, but I know I wouldn't see this at Temple Bible College." She struggled to remember what she had been taught about hating the sin but loving the sinners.

Sitting next to him, she could not understand why any girl did not like guys. She blushed when she said aloud, "I like guys."

Open mouth. Insert foot.

The sound of an ambulance drowned out the noise of the rally and the preacher, and gave Natalia a welcomed reason to be quiet. She wondered if the ambulance was for Gladys.

"I'd better go," she said over the siren. "I promised to get Gladys her clothes. Thanks for helping her. I'll see you later."

"I wasn't helping Gladys. I wanted to help you."

"You did?"

"Yes. As you were leaving, you looked like you needed help, and I wanted to be there for you."

So sweet.

"Can I give you a ride?" Nathan asked.

Natalia felt confused.

"You said you wanted to ride a motorcycle, said Nathan. "Mine's parked behind the psychology department. It will be quick. You'll like it."

"Well, okay. Why not? Do you have an extra helmet?"

"Yes, I have an extra helmet," he said, laughing. He stood up and offered his hand to help Natalia get up. They held hands as they walked back across campus toward the Quad.

Natalia was shaking as she put on the helmet and straddled the seat behind Nathan. She repeated to herself, *I've got this, I've got this, I've got this,* but it didn't work. Nathan reached behind, took her by the wrists, and wrapped her arms around his waist. He said, "Hold on tight." Natalia thought she might faint.

Natalia gasped when he accelerated out of the parking area. The sight of the road speeding by so close made her forget about Christian decorum. She squeezed him tight and pressed herself against his back as if her life depended on it.

Let me off!

"We'll take the long way," he shouted, "so you can get used to it."

"Okay," she croaked.

She felt certain that she would die. She felt tight – not just her grip on Nathan, but her stomach and lungs and heart felt like they were electrified. It was a little bit like when she was about to take an important penalty kick in a soccer tournament – a terrifying excitement that she wouldn't trade for anything. After a few minutes, when she realized that her death was not imminent, she was able to relax a little and pay attention to the experience. She did not loosen her grip, though. Her helmet was pressed sideways against Nathan's back, so she could see the

211

streets and buildings and people on the sidewalks, but she could not see where they were going.

She shouted, "This is fun," and she meant it.

Keep going.

Natalia thought about all the things that she was not allowed to do – the movies she couldn't watch, the music she couldn't listen to, the books she couldn't read, and the clothes she couldn't wear. Riding a motorcycle with a guy was certainly near the top of the list. She adjusted her grip around Nathan's waist. She felt like an adult – brave and able to make her own decisions.

Mom would die if she saw me now.

When Nathan reached highway speed on the road out of town, Natalia felt dizzy. The road and her thoughts were a blur.

What's the harm? It's not like I want to marry him. Maybe I can lead him to Jesus. Rachel is dating. Everybody is dating. So what if he's not a Christian?

She lost track of time. When they pulled up in front her dorm, Natalia didn't know if they'd been riding for five minutes or five hours. Nathan waited outside while Natalia packed Gladys' clothes in the army-green duffle bag. Nathan held the bag across his lap on the trip back, so Natalia had to hold him around his chest. He took a direct route back to the Student Center.

I want to take the long way again.

When they arrived, there was no ambulance, the rally was over, and the Cowboy was gone. Natalia waved as Nathan drove off. She could not stop smiling and she watched until he was out of sight. She would have kissed him on the cheek, but his helmet was in the way.

She sighed, turned, and walked into the Student Center.

As she rode the elevator to the Wellness Center, she saw her reflection in the polished metal elevator door. She was still smiling.

"Keep thy heart with all diligence; for out of it are the issues of life."

Her feelings toward Nathan were new and confusing and strong. Her guilt about those feelings was also strong.

Wipe that grin off your face, young lady. What are you thinking? You were enjoying a lot more than the motorcycle ride, young lady.

When the doors opened, Stephanie was back at her desk.

"Your friend is sleeping in Mrs. Hill's office," she said in greeting.

Natalia said, "She asked me to bring her some clothes. Would you see that she gets them?"

"Come with me. You can give them to her."

You should have been this helpful when I was here before, Natalia thought as she followed Stephanie down a long hallway.

Natalia felt guilty and sad and confused as Stephanie led her to an office where Gladys was asleep on a leather couch. She looked peaceful.

Stephane said, "They gave her medicine."

Natalia put the bag at her suitemate's feet and turned to leave. She took the stairs.

Chapter 20

I hope he's not doing paperwork today, thought Natalia as she walked toward the Quad. Fall had given way to a preview of winter. The sky was overcast and the wind ripped leaves from the trees.

I bet he rakes the leaves as quickly as they fall.

She wanted to talk to Box. She wanted to talk about Gladys, but mostly, she wanted to talk about Nathan.

Rachel was not returning her calls, and Natalia had to tell somebody that she had feelings for Nathan. She knew she should not date him. She was not sure what lust felt like, but she thought she might have felt it. Not lust in a sexual way – she had wanted to touch his face and to stare into his eyes and for him to touch her hair. She wanted him to kiss her.

I've got to tell somebody.

She hoped that if she told Box, he would set her straight.

No dates. Even if he asks – which he probably won't anyway – and no more motorcycle rides.

As she neared her bench on the Quad she saw a man raking leaves. For a second, she thought it was Box. But it was Sam, and she could see that he was crying. Natalia's thoughts snapped immediately back to

Gladys and the Student Union, to the gay pride rally and the street preacher, and somehow she knew that the ambulance she heard had been for Box.

Sam stopped raking, glanced at Natalia, and then stared at the leaves. "Is he all right?" Natalia asked with hesitation.

Sam shook his head. "He died, ma'am. I'm sorry."

Natalia gasped and covered her mouth with her hands. She felt faint. Again.

He was just here.

Sam shook his head again, turned away, and resumed raking.

He didn't get to go back to Yellowstone.

She stood and watched Sam rake.

I liked Box.

Sam paused, and then turned to Natalia. Fighting back more tears, he said, "I loved that man. He led me to the Lord."

I loved him, too.

Chapter 21

Nathan had never been to a funeral and this was only the second time he had been inside a church. He scanned the packed rows for Natalia. He found her and squeezed in beside her.

They had to sit even closer than when doing the puppet shows, but not as close as on his motorcycle; in either case, she had not worn a little black dress with a pearl necklace and matching earrings and nice perfume. Her hair was longer than he remembered and seemed to glow as it gently curled over her dress and pale shoulders.

He wondered about funeral etiquette. *Is it okay to tell someone they look hot at a funeral?*

"Hi," he whispered.

"Hi," she whispered back.

"You look nice. That's a pretty dress."

"Thank you."

"It wouldn't reach the floor, would it?" he asked with smile as he glanced at her legs.

She frowned.

"Your hair – it's pretty, down like that."

"Thank you," she said, but she did not look at him.

He decided it was *not* okay to tell someone at a funeral that they looked hot. He sat quietly and looked around. When he sensed Natalia was looking the other way, he stole a glance at her legs or her hair.

Beautiful.

The stained-glass windows of the sanctuary were huge – at least twice as tall as the plain-glass windows in the basement of the psychology building. The stained-glass depicted scenes of people and animals, but Nathan did not recognize most of them. He knew the guy on the cross was Jesus.

So, that's what Jesus looks like.

There was a large portrait of Henry Brown behind an open coffin. Flowers surrounded both. Nathan could not see the body. He had never seen a dead body and did not think he wanted to.

The choir, in their long purple robes, filed in behind the coffin and began to sing. He noticed that some in the choir could not sing – they just stood there and cried. He recognized Mrs. Weber. She was one of those who couldn't sing.

What's a bulwark?

Nathan had disagreed with Box about religion and politics, but he had liked him anyway. He had seemed genuinely nice and Nathan had enjoyed their talks. He had especially liked his stories about his days as a boxer and his time in Vietnam.

Nathan thought about the things Box had said. *"Jesus was who he said he was. You need Jesus, Nate. Follow the evidence, Nate."*

When Box had said, "I'm praying for you, Nate," Nathan had believed him.

Nathan noticed Dr. Weber seated in one of the folding chairs set up to hold the overflow crowd. He looked sick. Nathan had not seen much of Weber lately. For a man with an open door policy, he kept his closed a lot.

After the choir had finished their song, a man in a black robe with a white collar stood up front and thanked everyone for attending. He invited people to stand and share their thoughts and memories of Henry Brown. One by one, people stood and fought back tears and to tell stories about the nice things Box had done.

I had no idea. He was surprised to learn that Box had meant so much to so many people.

A young lady stood and told about when she had fallen on hard times and how Box had brought her food and fixed the fuel pump in her old car. An old man told about how Box had won a bronze medal in the Olympics. He told about how Box had almost been killed while dragging a wounded buddy to safety in Vietnam – he had been awarded a Purple Heart. Box's son stood and told everyone that Henry Brown was the best father and grandfather in the world. His daughter tried to share something, but she couldn't.

Why am I crying?

When it seemed no one else wanted to speak, the man in the black robe stood again.

He said, "Michelle, kids, family members, loved ones, and friends – we gather here today to honor and celebrate the life of Henry Moses Brown.

"Henry was born sixty-five years ago, on March the fifth, to Moses and Olive Brown, not too far from where we are now. His early years were hard and Henry had to fight to survive. We have already heard today about his sporting achievements, his military service, his family life, and his personal qualities. But I want to share with you what Henry Brown told me he wanted said in his eulogy. You see, Box knew he was dying."

A murmur ran through the room.

He knew?

The man paused to let the news sink in. When the murmurs subsided, he continued.

"Henry knew he was dying. Michelle and the kids knew, too, but he wanted to keep it quiet. He knew that if word got out that he had advanced pancreatic cancer, people would make a fuss. Henry came to my office about a month ago, after he got the diagnosis. He said, 'Pastor, I'm dying, and I want to help you write my eulogy.'"

A few of the mourners smiled and chuckled.

"He said, 'I've got cancer of the pancreas and the doctors say I've only got a few months left, and I've been thinking about what I want said at my funeral.' Needless to say, I was stunned, but when I regained my composure, I asked him. 'What do you want said at your funeral, Henry?' He said, 'If anybody shows up, pastor,'" and the pastors chuckled as he looked over the huge crowd, "'If anybody shows up, I want you to talk about Jesus. Don't talk about me. Talk about Jesus.' So here it goes."

Nathan stopped trying to look at Natalia and listened as the pastor talked about Jesus. He had heard about Jesus before – Box had told him – but that day, now that Box was dead, the message seemed important. Nathan listened carefully.

God loves me and has a plan for my life. All have sinned and fall short of the glory of God. Jesus Christ is God's only provision for my sin. I must individually receive Jesus Christ as Savior and Lord.

"Henry told me to tell you," continued the pastor, "that if you haven't done it already, you need to personally accept Jesus as your personal Savior." Nathan frowned. *No I don't.* But he kept listening.

The pastor took a deep breath, smiled, and said, "I did it. I kept my word and said what Henry told me to say. But I didn't promise him that was ALL I would say." There was more chuckling.

He's dead and they're laughing.

"And if Henry Brown has a problem with that, he'll have to take it up with me when I see him again in heaven!"

Heaven?

Nathan had never believed he was immortal, but it was the first time he really wondered what happened to him when he died.

The pastor said, "I could not stand here today and talk about this man without telling you what he meant to me. You see, even pastors go through dry spots. A few years after I came to Calvary Way, I was in a dry and barren place spiritually. I doubted my calling and was thinking about quitting the ministry. Henry came to my office. It was the middle of the day and he was in his work uniform. He said, 'Pastor, God just put it on my heart to pray for you, and that's what I'm here to do.' And even though it was hard for him, because of his back, he got right down on his knees and he prayed. It made a difference."

I'm praying for you Nate.

The pastor paused to take a drink of water. He looked at the people in the front row and said, "Henry Brown isn't dead. He is more alive than ever. Michelle, Henry, Rebecca, Sarah, Elijah, Noah, and Mary, he loved you very much. He prayed for you every single day."

He looked across the rest of the audience and said, "And if you ever met Henry Brown, you can rest assured that he prayed for you, too. State University was his mission field. His message, the message of Jesus, was not welcome there, but that did not stop him. When they tried to make him stop, he did not. When they tried to get him fired, he did not stop. When they mocked him, he prayed for his mockers."

Nathan felt sorry for the time that he had joined the gang at *Papa Joe's* and mocked the Cowboy.

"There was one more thing Henry asked me to do. He asked me to read from Hebrews 8:10. I am not sure why he chose that verse, but I know he had his reasons. It says 'I will put my laws in their minds and write them on their hearts. I will be their God.'"

"I will put my laws in their minds and write them on their hearts." Nathan repeated to himself. He felt a knot in the pit of his stomach. His mind raced and he did not hear anything else.

Box made him say that for me.

He felt light-headed, like he might faint. Nathan remembered when he had explained the baby study to Box. Box had said, "Nate, those little babies are just like us – you and me. They will try to choose the good. That is God's law – it is written on our hearts from the beginning. But like us, they'll be selfish and mean little beasts, too. You'll see."

Written on the heart?

He took the Bible from the back of the pew in front of him and looked at the table of contents for Hebrews.

For this is the covenant that I will make with the house of Israel after those days, saith the Lord; I will put my laws into their mind, and write them in their hearts: and I will be to them a God, and they shall be to me a people: And they shall not teach every man his neighbor, and every man his brother, saying, Know the Lord: for all shall know me, from the least to the greatest. For I will be merciful to their unrighteousness, and their sins and their iniquities will I remember no more.

It dawned on Nathan that perhaps every psychologist in history had been wrong about human morality.

The Bible *was right*! He had shown in the lab that infants, too young to sit up straight, have a moral compass.

It is built-in, just like the Bible says.

He felt guilty.

"All have sinned, Nate. That is why we all need Jesus."

He had questions and needed to talk to somebody.

Not Natalia.

As soon as he heard the pastor say, "Amen, thank you for coming," Nathan slipped out of the pew and headed toward the front of the church.

I need to talk to Mrs. Weber.

Chapter 22

The last place the distinguished professor Ernst Weber wanted to be was in a church at the funeral of that crazy Christian gardener who had brainwashed his wife. However, when the president of the university had sent an 'all staff' email announcing Henry Brown's funeral, Weber had he felt obligated to attend.

Dr. Weber sat in a folding chair at the end of a pew near the back of the church. *I am glad he's dead,* he thought.

Dr. Weber had been inside many churches. He had been confirmed in the Catholic Church when he was seven, and he had attended Mass twice a week until he was sixteen, the year he had become an atheist. Since then, he had been to countless weddings and funerals. He recognized the scenes depicted in the stained glass – the Ten Commandments, Moses parting the Red Sea, Noah and his ark, the miraculous conception, mean old Pontius Pilate, the crucifixion, the resurrection, and the second coming.

Myths for weak-minded simpletons.

He listened and rolled his eyes as people stood and told stories about how the wonderful Henry Brown.

He may have been nice, but that does not make him less crazy.

One after another, they praised Henry Brown. Weber tried to tune them out.

Henry Brown this and Henry Brown that.

He tried not to wonder about what people would say at *his* funeral. He tried not to care. Dr. Weber fidgeted and adjusted his necktie, and wondered if he could leave without being seen.

When someone said, "He's in heaven now," or "He's in a better place," Dr. Weber clenched his fists.

He is dead. Get over it.

When the pastor said that Henry knew he was dying, the corner of Weber's mouth pulled back in a quick little snarl.

If his god is real, why did he give him cancer?

He tried not to look at his wife – standing up there in her choir robe, wiping tears from her eyes. But he had to look when it was Elizabeth Weber who stood to speak.

Sit down, Elizabeth, please!

She did not sit. Instead, she wiped away the tears, glanced her husband's way, and said, "I owe Henry Brown my life."

No, you do not.

She took a deep breath and exhaled slowly. "I tried to get him fired for talking about Jesus. I was Saul. I was a fool. I persecuted Henry Brown. And do you know what he said? He said, 'I'm praying for you, Elizabeth.' He never gave up. He helped me to see the evidence for God and for Jesus – and it made sense. I was tired of hating Henry, tired of running from God, and tired of hiding my sin and doubt. We prayed together on a bench on the Quad. Henry Box Brown led me to Christ, and I'll never forget him for that."

Neither will I.

Dr. Weber remembered the day. He had watched from the window of his corner office. He had seen Henry and his wife on the bench, holding hands, heads bowed. He had known what had happened and he had felt sick.

He almost allowed himself to consider that he was wrong and Elizabeth and Box were right. They were both so sure. He almost allowed himself to remember that he had once believed – when he was young – before his mother had died. He had been sure, too. He almost let himself think about the evidence for Jesus. He almost thought, for a second, that Henry Brown had perhaps not been an ignorant, naïve, gullible, fundamentalist wacko. He almost thought about the possibility that his life and his career spent disproving God was a big fat lie. But the pain pills were kicking in, so he didn't think about it anymore.

Chapter 23

When she was little, Natalia had thought that you could measure a person's importance in life by the number of people who attended their funeral when they died. When a police officer, important business leader, or young child died, the sanctuary at First Baptist was full. She had known that Pastor Galloway was very important because, at his funeral, the deacons had needed to set up extra chairs to accommodate all the mourners.

If the number of people at the Henry Brown's funeral was a measure of his worth, he was the most important person she had ever met.

I had no idea, she thought. She found a pew with room for two.

The pews were filling fast and she didn't know if she could keep her promise to save a seat for Nathan. She felt sad that Box had died. She felt nervous seeing Nathan again.

As she scanned the sanctuary for Nathan, Natalia recognized one of the men in black suits setting up folding chairs in the aisle – it was the street preacher. He looked like a regular guy without the cowboy hat.

It was not Natalia's first funeral. She had been to dozens with her mom -- maybe a hundred. Her mom always said it was important to pay your respects, offer condolences, sign the guest book, and bring a comforting casserole.

Natalia preferred funerals in a church, like this one, to graveside services or visitation at the funeral home. Church funerals were usually like a regular church service – just sadder. Once, Natalia had went with her mom to a funeral at Abundant Life Fellowship, a charismatic country church. It had not been at all like a regular church service. During the eulogy, the pastor had shouted and cried and pounded the lid of the coffin with his shoe and yelled, "Sweet Jesus! Sweet Jesus!" Then he had taken off his other shoe and walked on the backs of the pews while he preached. He hadn't even stumbled. Natalia had thought she would like to walk on the backs of the pews, but had known better than to try.

Graveside services were usually shorter, but sometimes they were hot and buggy and it was hard to hear. It was visitation, also called viewing, that she really did not like. She did not like having to look at the body and then say something nice to the family. She was afraid the body would move, and she never knew what to say to the family.

"I'm sorry for your loss."

She saw Nathan. He looked uncomfortable in his tie and blue blazer. She gave a little wave when he looked in her direction. When he squeezed in the pew beside her, she had to put her hands in her lap to make enough room.

"Hi," he whispered.

"Hi," she replied.

I'll tell him after, she promised herself. She was not going to be dramatic. She would just tell him that she had had fun and he was a great guy, but that she was not ready to date anybody.

"You look nice. That's a pretty dress." He whispered.

"Thank you." He smelled clean – like shampoo.

"It wouldn't pass a modesty check, would it?" he asked.

He's checking me out.

"Your hair. It's pretty like that."

It's a funeral, not a date. Eyes front, buddy!

"Thank you," she said instead.

She pointed out Dr. Weber to Nathan. She thought he looked sick.

After the choir filed in, they sang, *A Mighty Fortress*. The director said it was Box's favorite. They left a gap in the back row where Box always stood.

A mighty fortress is our God, a bulwark never
failing;
Did we in our own strength confide, our striving
would be losing?

Mrs. Weber and several of the others couldn't finish the song. It made Natalia sad when she saw people struggle to sing or speak at funerals or weddings. If anyone broke down and sobbed, Natalia did, too.

There was plenty of sobbing as one by one people stood and told their own story about what Henry Box Brown had meant to them.

I barely knew him. She remembered Mr. Allen. She felt shallow – that she hadn't known him very well either.

Natalia was not too surprised to learn that Box knew he was dying.

I thought he looked tired.

She imagined Box telling the pastor what to say at his own funeral. She was glad she hadn't known that Box was dying.

I wouldn't know what to say.

Suddenly, she missed her mom. She missed Rachel, too.

She was relieved when the pastor said, "Let us pray." It was a signal that the service was almost over and a chance for Natalia to compose herself – to stuff her emotions and wipe away the tears.

Instead, God spoke to her again – directly to her mind. She heard Him with her heart as certainly as she had heard the pastor with her ears.

And ye shall seek me, and find me, when ye shall search for me with all your heart.

She felt guilty.

I haven't been searching.

She prayed.

I'm sorry.

She felt relief wash over her.

What was I thinking?

She promised God that she would pray all the time, as she used to, and read the Bible every day.

It's just that simple.

After the pastor said, "Amen," Natalia took a deep breath.

And no more dating non-believers.

She wiped her eyes, and turned to tell Nathan that they needed to talk, but he was already gone.

Chapter 24

Two weeks after Box's funeral, on the first day of fall break, Natalia's dorm, like the rest of State University, seemed empty and quiet. Her suitcase was packed with dirty clothes and her backpack had the books that she needed to study for midterms. Her dad was on his way to pick her up for the long drive home. She looked forward to seeing him. She looked forward to a week at home – to sleeping in her bed, eating her mom's cooking, and hanging out with Rachel.

She looked forward to telling her mom that she had decided to work in AWANA at Calvary Way.

Approved workmen are not ashamed, she reminded herself.

She was nervous about telling her parents about Nathan, so she practiced again.

Mom and Dad, I met this guy. His name is Nathan.

I think you will like him.

Yes, he is a Christian, Mom.

It was the Sunday after the funeral when Natalia found out that Nathan was saved. He had been wearing his blue blazer and was standing with Mrs. Weber in the hall outside of the College and Career

Sunday school classroom. He had looked nervous. He had said, "I bet you're surprised to see me here."

Natalia had thought, *Dr. Weber is dead.* Why else would Nathan be there with Mrs. Weber? Everyone knew that after the funeral, Dr. Weber had gotten a DUI and had checked himself into rehab.

Now he is dead.

"Did something bad happen?" Natalia had asked.

"No," Nathan had laughed. "I'm a Christian."

Did not see that coming.

Natalia had felt like squealing. She had touched Nathan's arm and said, "That's wonderful! When? What happened?"

"First," he had said, "I'm sorry for running out after Box's funeral. Something happened. When the pastor read the verse from Hebrews – 'I will put my laws in their hearts, and I will write them on their minds' – I kept thinking about the babies in the study. There *is* a law written in their little minds. I felt challenged. It was like, if the Bible is right about our moral core, what else is it right about? I had all these questions in my head and my chest was tight. I know I could have talked to you, but…" He had paused and looked at the floor. "My intentions with you have not been exactly pure – but that's another story."

Yes! She had resisted the urge to say, *Now I can date you.*

Instead, Natalia had put on her best *I've got this* face.

Nathan had continued, "I heard Mrs. Weber talk about how she persecuted Christians, so I wanted to ask her some questions." He had looked at Mrs. Weber, who continued the story.

"I wanted to talk with my husband. During the service, he looked sick. But he left the funeral in a hurry. Nathan found me in the parking lot and we went for coffee. He had questions about what I believed and why," she had explained.

"I had a *lot* of questions," Nathan had interjected.

"I answered them as best I could, and to make a long conversation short," she had looked at Nathan and smiled warmly, "He invited Christ into his heart to be his Lord and Savior."

He had looked to Natalia like a proud little boy when he said, "And now I'm going to join your class. If that's all right."

All right?

"Of course it's all right. That's great," she had said.

"Maybe I can give you a ride home after class?"

"Sure. Why not?"

Her reminiscing was interrupted when she saw her dad arrive in the family mini-van. She felt like a little girl again and her dad was picking her up after a week at summer camp. She gave him a big hug. He told his old joke about dirty laundry.

As they drove, they talked about her classes and grades and the people back home.

"My classes are going good. I'm making all As."

"Your mother is excited. She is making a feast."

"The food's pretty good, Dad. I think I'm getting fat."

"Your brother is fine. He's playing goalie this year."

Natalia felt comfortable and safe with her dad. She realized that one of the things she had liked about Box was the way he had made her feel comfortable and safe, too.

When they pulled into the driveway, her mom ran out and immediately started to cry. Her dad was ready with a tissue.

Her brother gave Natalia his sly smile and said, "Hi Gnat, have you been gone?"

"I know you must be starving," her mom said after she blew her nose. "You look like you haven't eaten much in three months. I made your favorite – broccoli and cheese casserole."

Her mom and dad and little brother took turns asking questions about college.

"What's your favorite food in the cafeteria?"

"What's your favorite class?"

"Did you get homesick?"

Her mom asked, "What happened to that girl, your suite mate – the one you asked for us to pray for?"

"The one with the flashy mom," her dad added.

Natalia remembered Gladys staring at her in the dark with her bloodshot eyes and bad breath. "She got sick, Mom. She was supposed to be on medication but she didn't take them. She started hearing voices and acting strange."

Her brother said, "Cool!" proving he was still annoying.

"It wasn't cool. She had to go to the hospital. I thought she would be back in a few days. But the resident assistant came and said that she Gladys withdrew from school. I don't know what happened.

I sent her a friend request on Facebook, but she hasn't replied."

Her mom said, "Bless her heart."

Sometimes when her mom blessed someone's heart, it irritated Natalia. When she said it, it sounded to Natalia like she was looking down on people – judging them. But this time Natalia wasn't irritated. She was happy to be home.

"My psychology teacher had some kind of breakdown too," Natalia said. "He had to go to rehab."

Her brother said, "Cool!" again, this time getting himself sent to his room.

"I rode a motorcycle," she said.

"Cool!" her brother shouted from the stairs.

Like drinking, dating, and dressing immodestly, her mom was opposed to motorcycles.

"You know how I feel about motorcycles," she said with a sigh and a frown. "But you're an adult now."

That went well.

"You would have liked my Sunday school teacher," Natalia said. "We called him Box. He was like a cross between Dad and Mr. Allen. That reminds me! I signed up to work in AWANA on Wednesdays."

Changing the subject from motorcycles to Sunday school and AWANA worked.

Her mom clapped her hands and said, "That's great, Natty Rose! What made you change your mind?"

I was being a lazy Christian and playing with fire, and God called me on it.

"I just decided I wanted to," she said, sure that her mom was reading her mind.

"...Mom and Dad," she announced as she twisted her purity ring around her finger.

Here it goes.

"It happened," she said.

Your little girl is all grown up.

"I met this guy. His name is Nathan. I think you'll like him – and yes, he is a Christian."

The End.

For Discussion

What feelings might you have as you go to college?

How will college be different than high school?

How will you make friends?

How can you respond to attacks on your worldview? Respond to, "Faith is belief despite lack of evidence."

How will you handle the new freedom of life at college?

How will relationships at home change when you go?

How might professors and classmates react when they learn you were homeschooled?

Will it be difficult living out your faith in college?

Explain your beliefs about Darwinian evolution.

Is the Astonishing Hypothesis astonishing to you?

In college, will there be pressure to conform?

What attitudes, beliefs, or behaviors will you be pressured to change?

How will you maintain spiritual discipline at college?

What would you do for a friend using drugs or alcohol?

What would you do for a friend with an eating disorder?

What would you do for a friend using internet porn?

What would you do for a friend who was thinking about cutting or killing himself or herself?

What would you do for a friend whose parents were divorcing?

Can you effectively and efficiently explain the reasons for your faith?

www.ingramcontent.com/pod-product-compliance
Lightning Source LLC
Chambersburg PA
CBHW070919180626
46817CB00003B/1130